The Richest Man or  Bradley's adventures previous works include *The Astronaut's Apprentice, City of Meteors,* and a lost masterpiece called *A Cow in the Canteen.*

You can reach the author by sending an e-mail to philipthreadneedle@falconberger.co.uk.

THE RICHEST
MAN ON MARS

BY PHILIP THREADNEEDLE

Falcon Berger

A Falcon Berger book
www.falconberger.com
published by arrangement with the author

ISBN: 1494256177
ISBN-13: 978-1494256173

Set in fonts created by Ray Larabie
www.larabiefonts.com

10 9 8 7 6 5 4 3 2 1

This book is dedicated to

my brothers, Ian and Adam,

with love

CHAPTERS

THE MOSQUITOES OF MARS

ONE DAY, WHILE Mercury and the giant white sun were shrinking behind them, Bradley decided that they should all have a house meeting.

It was not a large spaceship, and nor was it a large crew. They gathered weightlessly by the console and waited for Bradley to begin. Grandpa was present—it was his spaceship, after all—and so too was a girl called Headlice. She came from Pluto and only had one eye, which shone beneath her fringe like bright blue Neptune.

"Well?" she demanded. "Why are we having a meeting?"

Bubbling quietly beside her, encased in a thick glass dome, was a wrinkled grey brain. Odder still, the brain had a giant nose stuck directly to the front of it.

"Seconded!" said the brain in a robotic voice. *"Further clarification would be most welcome!"*

This strange aquatic creature was known as Captain Nosegay. He seldom spoke but used his prodigious nostrils to help them navigate.

"All right, all right!" muttered Bradley. "Give me chance!"

He paused to gather his thoughts. They had so much to discuss. Worst of all, there was a burning question that he didn't dare ask, but which had been rolling round his brain since the day he'd left Earth.

He looked at the ceiling for inspiration. Floating high above his head was the last crew member: a worried-looking (but no less adorable) ball of fluff called Waldo. Waldo was a star-pup, which made him one of the only creatures in the universe to reproduce by exploding. He had no arms or legs and simply floated around the cabin, minding his own business.

Bradley let his eyes wander from Waldo to one

of the portholes. Floating outside was a constellation of cold stars, and in the middle was a single very bright one that must have been a comet. It shone like white gold, spreading a peacock's tail of ghostly rays.

"Bradley?" said Headlice.

He didn't answer. All around the comet, the darkness seemed to intensify.

"Bradley?" said Headlice again.

He shook his head to clear it. He'd gone all strange for a moment.

"Okay," he said suddenly. "I'm starting the meeting. Basically, there are a couple of things we need to discuss."

He paused, thinking that the spaceship seemed weirdly empty. Only days earlier, there'd been another crew member: a blue-skinned alien called Wuztop Nash. Before joining them to hunt treasure, Wuztop had lived on an asteroid, making gentlemen's space suits to order.

Sadly, he was no longer with them. Annoyed by their failure to find riches, he'd gone off in a huff and decided to stay on Mercury.

Suddenly, Grandpa rolled his eyes and groaned.

"So much for starting the meeting!" he said.

Bradley blushed and got on with it.

"All right—well we need to talk about me going home," he said. "I've been in space for weeks now. I've missed *four lots* of pocket money. I mean, don't get me wrong," he assured them—"it's not about the money—it's fifty pee. But Dad always finds me a shiny new coin to have."

"Well can't he wire you the funds?" wondered Grandpa.

"Well no," said Bradley wearily. "We're in space. But even if he *could* send me money, I've got school to think about. I can't bunk off forever. I'll end up like Charlie Masterson!"

"Who's Charlie Masterson?" asked Headlice.

Bradley groaned. He shouldn't have said that. Now he'd have to go off on a tangent.

"He was in hospital for months," he explained. "He got behind on his school work and had to stay down a year. Now he gets bullied."

"Well *that's* not nice," said Headlice.

Bradley held up his hands.

"Look. Don't shoot the messenger," he told her. "*I* don't bully him. I got a black eye once, thank you very much, for trying to stick up for him! But anyway—that's not the most important thing."

He paused and took a deep breath. There was a question that he needed to ask. He wanted to ask it, but was so very frightened of the answer.

"The most important thing—" he began.

He stopped again. It was too hard.

For a second, he was transported back in time to the fateful night when he first saw his mother's face.

She had died when he was a baby. Instead of burying her, his father had put her into *suspended animation*, which meant that she was frozen in a sort of capsule back on Earth. The idea must have been to bring her back to life one day, and for all Bradley knew, that was possible. After all, Dad's own father—the intrepid astronaut that Bradley knew as Grandpa—was an alien. And who knew what alien technology could achieve?

Bradley had seen all kinds of wizardry since leaving Earth. It wasn't unthinkable that Grandpa could help. But Bradley had been travelling with Grandpa for a while now, and hadn't worked up the courage to broach the topic.

So the question that Bradley needed to ask— the question that burned like a hot coal in the back of his mind, glowing whenever his thoughts blew across it—was whether Grandpa could bring his mother back to life.

But what if he couldn't?

"It doesn't matter," he decided at last— instantly hating himself for chickening out. "We can talk about it later. Basically, I ran away from home. I've got no idea what trouble I'm in, or what school thinks about it, and—and that's it."

He paused. He felt suddenly very weak. When he swallowed, his throat was raw and dry.

"And I think I'm getting ill," he added. "I feel rotten, and my head went funny a moment ago."

His eyes wandered back to the portholes. Space normally seemed beautiful—so unspeakably magical—but instead it looked cold and unlovely. It was like a black ocean under a sheet of dark ice. Their little ship was caught in a slow current, going absolutely nowhere.

The comet was still looking through the window. It seemed to wink, but not in a friendly way.

"Bradley?" said Grandpa. "Are you okay?"

He tried to answer. Instead, his vision swam. He realised very quickly that something was wrong. The comet seemed to be laughing at him, and the dreadful sound rang in his ears as he slipped into unconsciousness.

After that, he was whirling in a dark void. It was as if the spaceship had cracked open like a giant egg, exposing him to the vacuum.

He went spinning away into cold dark space, wondering what on Earth had happened, and when and how he would ever wake up.

Luckily, after a long time—maybe hours or days or even weeks—he came to in a strange round bed in a strange glassy bubble.

When he sat up, he saw that the bubble was one of many, joined by a tangle of tubes that were wide enough to walk down.

Because the walls were see-through, he had a good view of the whole complex—which, as far as he could tell, was orbiting high above a cloud-covered planet.

His own bubble was on the outer edges of the network. In the middle was a much bigger one, with strange flying machines chugging this way and that inside it. Orbiting the top of this central bubble, turning slowly like a sort of halo, were flashing red words that told the name and purpose of the complex. *The World Famous Orbiting Hospital!* they boasted. *Venus's One and*

Only Satellite, Est. 1881 for the Good of All.

Hospital. He really *was* ill.

Having just woken up, he was surprised that he didn't need a wee. When he lifted the duvet, he was astonished and dismayed to see that he was wearing a sort of enormous white nappy (or *diaper*, as they say in the US and on Grabelon). He let the duvet fall and tried not to think about it.

"Hello?" he called—looking down the tube that joined his bubble to the rest. "Is anyone there?"

Before long, a strange figure floated into view. Bradley guessed that she was a doctor. She wore a white coat and was riding a sort of flying scooter. Her face was the colour of grass, and her hair—if you could call it that— was like stringy green moss that dangled by her cheeks. Most striking of all were her eyes, which (in sharp contrast to the rest of her) were a vivid red colour. They twinkled in her face like dark rubies.

"You're awake!" she observed in a shrill voice.

"At last! You missed your visitors, I'm afraid. They said they'd be back tomorrow."

He was heartbroken.

"Tomorrow?" he echoed. "You mean—you mean they didn't want to stay?"

But she just snorted.

"Of course they did!" she assured him. "But we have strict visiting hours here. I kicked them out an hour ago. Do you know what's wrong with you?"

He shook his head.

"Well I'm sorry to say it's bad news," she told him gravely. "You've had a full-blown case of *space malaria.* You must have been bitten by a Martian mosquito!"

He was surprised to hear this.

"But I've never even *been* to Mars," he told her. "We just flew over it. We didn't even leave the spaceship."

"So? *You're* from Earth," she pointed out. "Yet here you are, high above the clouds of Venus. The mosquitoes of Mars travel too. You could have been bitten anywhere. Would you like to see one?"

His curiosity got the better of him.

"Go on," he said—sitting up a bit. "Show me."

She pulled out a transparent plastic pot. Inside was a blue-green mosquito, whose wings were as bright as polished turquoise. It was much bigger than an Earth mosquito. It had a long sharp needle for a mouth, and enormous eyes like clusters of sapphires.

Bradley was horrified.

"I think I would have noticed *that*," he told her. "It's bigger than my thumb!"

"Well yes," said the doctor. "But watch this!"

She gave the pot a light shake, startling the mosquito. It began to change colour, flashing pink and orange and snow white. Finally, it flickered in a strange way and vanished altogether.

"The mosquitoes of Mars are masters of disguise," she explained. "Sadly, this one's *camouflage* has gone a bit haywire. That's why he's here. We've put him on a course of very small tablets."

Bradley folded his arms in annoyance.

"Well I don't know why you're even treating him," he told her. "Not if they go around making people ill!"

But the doctor shook her head, then pointed through the skin of the bubble—to the flashing red words that turned in the distance.

"For the good of all," she reminded him. "That's our motto. We don't take sides, young man. Now get some rest. I'll be back later," she promised, "to update your notes and change your nappy."

She went off on her flying scooter. Bradley lay back and stared at the stars. Before long, he was fast asleep, dreaming of wild white horses on a Martian plain.

THE WATERS OF TITANIA

LIFE IN THE orbiting hospital was far from unbearable, but nor was it a non-stop party.

As far as views went, Venus was not that striking. However, over time, Bradley came to appreciate its subtle charms. The clouds reminded him of sweet frothy foam on a cappuccino. Sometimes, veins of blue lightning would flash across them, forking and racing this way and that.

Other times, dark shapes would be seen in the whippy clouds. When she was doing her rounds, the doctor explained that these were floating towns, submerged beneath the dense atmosphere.

"That one's Upton-on-Air," she said, pointing it out. It was smaller than the others, and through the cloud, faint blue lights could be seen all over it. "My cousin owns a restaurant there. If you like cloudfish curry, you won't find a better meal in all the skies of Venus!"

Sadly, the hospital food didn't stretch as far as cloudfish curry. Nonetheless, it was as weird and as wonderful as you might expect. Meals were delivered in foil trays, and each would be a lucky dip of silver peas, sweet purple bread, sliced green meat, brilliant blue beans, and countless other exotic treats. Bradley didn't have much of an appetite, but ate what he could and nibbled the rest. Once the doctor saw he was getting stronger, she agreed that he could walk to the nearest toilet rather than wearing a nappy.

The first morning that Bradley was awake, Grandpa and Headlice came to visit. Grandpa looked awful. He had bags under his eyes. His magnificent moustache, which was normally groomed to perfection, was all over the place. Nonetheless, his face lit up when he saw his grandson.

"Bradley!" he cried. "I've been *so* worried about you! Worried sick! By the Great Red Spot of Jupiter! Space malaria is a serious business—make no mistake about it! How are you feeling?"

"Up and down," said Bradley. "I'm not too bad right now. How are you?"

"Oh, fine, fine," said Grandpa—and they began to talk about this and that thing. After a while, the doctor came to take Bradley's temperature. She heard them talking about returning to Earth and quickly quashed the idea.

"No chance," she said flatly. "They've never had space malaria there, so we can't risk contamination. You won't be allowed to return until it's completely out of your system. Earth is a protected nature reserve, you know!"

"A *nature* reserve?" said Bradley in disbelief. "How is Earth a *nature* reserve?"

"Well from *our* point of view," said the doctor, "it's almost completely untouched. A primitive backwater. People don't want to spoil it, so it was declared a nature reserve and that's that."

Bradley folded his arms in annoyance.

"If it's a primitive backwater," he pointed out, "then why does everyone in space speak English?"

The doctor laughed.

"Well, we wanted a universal language," she explained. "The Martians suggested Martian, but no one else thought that was fair. In the end, we decided to pick a neutral language that no one had heard of. Naturally, we looked to Earth for such an obscure dialect. It was going to be Mandarin Chinese," she added with a sigh, "but no one could get the hang of it—and anyway—backwater or not—I'm afraid you simply *can't* return until you're completely cured."

Bradley groaned in frustration.

"Well what do I do now?!" he wondered.

"Get better," said the doctor simply. "That's your top priority. I'm going to put you on a course of water. Half a thimbleful, three times a day. I'll bring you the first cup later."

"Oh, brilliant," said Bradley sarcastically.

"Homeopathy. Just what I need."

The doctor didn't look amused.

"It's not *any* old water," she told him. "Trust an Earthling not to know that! It's from Titania. The waters there are full of all kinds of helpful micro-organisms. They'll make you better in no time!"

They continued to talk about this or that thing. Eventually, they decided that Grandpa would have to go to Earth and tell Dad what had happened to delay them in space. The old man seemed nervous about facing the music.

"They won't be pleased to see me!" he pointed out. But all the same, he agreed to do it.

After the visitors left, Bradley got on with the business of getting better.

It wasn't long before the doctor brought the first of his treatments. He was disappointed to see that the micro-organisms weren't quite as "micro" as he'd hoped. In fact, there were little blue specks swimming this way and that in the water.

"Just drink it," said the doctor.

He did, and was surprised when it fizzed in his mouth like sherbet.

She didn't hang around, so Bradley had to entertain himself. Life in the orbiting bubble had the potential to be very boring. There was a sort of floating telly, which hovered in from time to time, but it only showed adverts. The doctor had explained that this was how the hospital paid for itself. People gave them money to put their ads on the telly, so sometimes, it would come in shouting, *Gee Whiz Soda! Taste the gravity!* Other times, it showed Len Zing's latest range of sofas, which you could buy on interest-free credit.

That evening, it tried to sell Bradley a sensational-sounding book called *The Andromeda Club Exposed.* This made him sit up and pay attention. Not long ago, they'd gone head to head with the Andromeda Club in a race for lost treasure. Bradley and Grandpa had found it first, and it wasn't anything exciting—just an ice-making machine, in fact—but he had no idea whether the Andromeda Club knew that. For all he knew, they were still angry and trying to hunt them down.

"Who exactly *are* the Andromeda Club?" demanded the telly, floating at the foot of his bed. "What goes on at their clubhouse? Where does all their money come from? What's *Project Vortex*, and why is the richest man on Mars so tight-lipped about it?"

Bradley had never even *heard* of Project Vortex—let alone wondered what it was. Of course, the telly didn't provide any answers— you had to buy the book to get those—so that was the extent of the diversion.

Luckily, Grandpa had left a stash of good novels. Between bouts of fever, Bradley sat up reading *Charlie and the Chocolate Factory, A Bad Spell for the Worst Witch,* the *Just William* series, and *A Cow in the Canteen.* It occurred to him that, when he returned to Earth, he could write a book of his own, inspired by his adventures in space.

Before long—as the sun began to set into the

creamy white clouds—he began to feel very tired. He put his book aside, closed his eyes, and fell fast asleep.

The next morning, Grandpa and Headlice returned. Bradley smiled to see them, but for some reason, Headlice wouldn't look at him.

"Well—I'm back!" said Grandpa proudly. "I did it!"

Bradley stiffened nervously.

"Already?" he said quickly. "What happened? Am I in trouble for running away?"

"Not at all!" beamed Grandpa, brushing his fears aside. "They were perfectly relaxed about it. Your father, for instance, was the very picture of cool-headedness. A model of patience."

Bradley was taken aback. It sounded too good to be true.

"Really?" he said. "They were *perfectly relaxed?*"

He tried to catch Headlice's eye. Every time he looked over, she stared unhappily at her feet.

After a while, he gave up and returned his attention to Grandpa.

"And you *definitely* went to Earth?" he said.

"Cross my heart," said Grandpa.

"And you *definitely* saw Dad and Grandma?"

"I most certainly did, young man. Saw 'em with my own two eyes. I distinctly remember," he added helpfully, "that your father was standing up."

"And what were they doing when you arrived?"

Grandpa looked skyward for inspiration. He seemed to be drawing on his extensive knowledge of Earth customs, trying to invent something believable.

At last, he clicked his fingers.

"They were robbing a bank," he said confidently.

Bradley groaned.

"Oh, Grandpa! You *haven't* been to Earth at all!" he said in disgust. "I can't *believe* you chickened out!"

The second they were rumbled, Headlice

rounded on Grandpa. Clearly, she hadn't enjoyed being part of the ruse.

"I *told* you not to lie!" she reminded him crossly. "Now let's go to Earth. Right now! Come on—chop chop!"

"All right, all right," said Grandpa unhappily.

She marched him out of the bubble and down the tubular corridor, and that was the last Bradley saw of them all day.

That afternoon, a curious thing happened to Bradley. He became feverish and passed out on the bed, tossing and turning in his sleep. In his mind, he was back on Grandpa's spaceship, and they were under attack.

The nightmare didn't come from his imagination. It was a memory of something real. During the outward journey, they'd been attacked by a gang of what Grandpa called *pirates*. They had powerful grey hands and bulging eyes, and jaws like those of the great white shark. Unlike all the other aliens they'd met, the pirates came from *outside the Solar*

System, and even Grandpa had been terrified of them.

Their leader—a brute with a scarred face—had nearly forced his way onto the spaceship. Luckily, Bradley had made him lose his grip and go tumbling away into space.

Now it was happening all over again—but this time, everything was going wrong. Headlice had been blown out through the whistling hatch. Grandpa was floating lifelessly by the console. And the pirate was coming for Bradley, with grasping grey hands that reached towards him...

He woke with a start, feeling dizzy and ill. His heart was pounding and his forehead was covered in cold sweat. Stranger still, the fever must have warped his perception of space, because it seemed as if the bed had grown enormously while he slept.

He heard the thin whine of the doctor's scooter.

"Doctor!" he cried weakly. "Doctor! I think

I'm delirious!"

"Why? What's up?"

He stretched his limbs in all directions. No matter how much he flailed about, he couldn't find the ends of the mattress.

"I had a nightmare," he complained, "and now it feels like the bed is enormous!"

"Well of course!" laughed the doctor. "You're not hallucinating. You've simply halved in size. It's a side effect of the treatment," she said matter-of-factly.

Bradley sat up and looked at her in horror. Only then did he realise how tiny he was. She was like a giant at the end of his gargantuan bed.

"I've *halved in size?*" he echoed. "Did you not think to *warn* me that I might *halve in size?!*"

She wasn't impressed.

"Oh, stop being such a cry-baby!" she said. "It'll only last a few hours. Unlike the colour change. I'm afraid *that* might turn out to be permanent."

He looked at her blankly, then cupped his ear.

"The *what*, sorry?" he said politely.

"The colour change. Haven't you looked in the mirror lately?"

He ignored her and lay down again. Everything seemed to be spinning. He held up his hands and saw, to his astonishment, that they had gone the colour of ripe blueberries. The idea of being half his normal size *and* a different colour was too much to bear. He simply refused to absorb the fact. In fact, he actually started to reject information that he'd already taken on board.

"It feels like the bed's enormous," he said again.

"It's not that," said the doctor firmly. "Like I said—you've just shrunk. Now get some sleep. When you feel a bit better, we'll talk about your new look."

The next day, when Grandpa and Headlice came to visit, they found Bradley staring at his face in a hand mirror. His hair was navy blue and his eyes sparkled like lapis lazuli. He'd returned to his normal size, but every inch of him was still a rich indigo colour.

Headlice gasped and clasped a hand to her mouth.

"Oh my word!" she squealed through her fingers. "Bradley! You look *so cute* in blue!"

"Sweet rings of Saturn!" croaked Grandpa. "What happened to you?!"

Bradley just sighed.

"It's a side effect of the treatment," he said bleakly. "I'm stuck with it for now. Maybe forever. Did you go back to Earth?"

Grandpa nodded unhappily, and Bradley knew immediately that he was telling the truth.

"Your father was *not* impressed with me," he muttered. "Not impressed at all. Gave me quite a dressing down! But you're not in trouble. Not with school, anyway. There's a doctor on Earth who knows I'm an alien. Your father got him to sign a letter saying you were in hospital."

Bradley puffed his cheeks out, then shrugged.

"Well it could have gone a lot worse," he

pointed out. "In fact, I can't see how it could have gone any better. I expected him to go totally ballistic. How did you pitch it?"

"I just assured him that you were turning out to be a very brave space explorer," replied Grandpa frankly, "and that he would be very proud of you if he could see how you were doing out here."

Bradley was touched and taken aback.

"You really said that?"

"I did. And it's true. I couldn't have asked for a better apprentice."

Bradley's face felt suddenly warm. He wondered if he was blushing. Then he wondered what colour his blushes would even be, now that he'd gone the colour of a blueberry.

Before he could dwell on that mystery for long, something else occurred to him. He wondered whether Dad had asked Grandpa to revive his frozen mother.

"Did he mention anything else?" he asked. "About—I don't know—about anything at all?"

Grandpa shook his head. He looked quite drained by the encounter.

"No," he said wearily. "He just went on about how irresponsible I was. He wants me to get you back to Earth as soon as possible, and in the meantime, he asked me to give you these fifty pence pieces."

When Bradley saw them, he knew that Grandpa was right. He really *wasn't* in trouble. He took the shiny new coins and put them in his bedside cabinet, which is exactly what he would have done with his pocket money back on Earth.

"Well I can hardly go back now," he said. "Look at me. I'm like a giant blueberry!"

Headlice sighed dreamily.

"Well *I* think you look amazing," she told him. "A real dreamboat!"

He didn't know how to respond to the compliment, so in the end, he just pretended he hadn't heard it. Then he got a fresh wave of nausea and buried his head in his hands.

Eventually, the doctor came chugging along

on her hovering scooter.

"Good news!" she said—reading some test results off a clipboard. "Bradley is on the mend. I can recommend we discharge him today, provided he doesn't visit Earth until he's got the all-clear. He still needs plenty of rest though. Do you know where he's going to spend his convalescence?"

"Not really," said Grandpa. "Can he spend it on a spaceship?"

"Depends. Does it have artificial gravity?"

"The sofa does," said Grandpa. "How's that?"

"Not great," warned the doctor. "He needs to build up his strength. Zero gee is bad for bone and bad for muscle! Can I recommend a convalescent care facility? I know an excellent one on Earth's moon..."

Bradley sat up at the mention of Earth's moon. In his current state, it was as close to home as he could reasonably get.

"It's called *Moon House*," continued the doctor. "It overlooks the Bay of Dew, just off the Ocean of Storms. You can't miss it!"

THE OCEAN OF STORMS

THE VERY NEXT day, they were racing over the grey rocky surface of the moon.

Bradley watched through a porthole. After so many surprises in space, he'd wondered if the moon would be swarming with flies or bright blue frogs. He'd even wondered if the so-called seas, which were just dark bits on the moon's surface, would turn out to be real rolling oceans.

But no. For once, there were no surprises. Bone-white craters gaped below. When they reached the so-called Ocean of Storms, it was just miles and miles of flat dark rock. In the sky above it—ripe and round like a blue-green berry—was planet Earth.

Bradley's heart sank. He couldn't go home—

that was for sure. Not since he'd changed colour. He'd have to stay in space. But what if he never went back to normal? Where would he live? What would he do...?

"Cheer up!" barked Grandpa from the console. "You haven't said anything for ages. You know *depression* is a secondary symptom of space malaria. Don't let it get to you!"

"Sorry," said Bradley automatically.

He returned his attention to planet Earth. All at once, with a sudden pang of emotion, he realised just how much he loved his home. It had never occurred to him before, but it was true. He loved the litter and the long grass. He loved the leaning goalposts and the wide dirty rivers. He loved the cars and coaches—the shining wet roads and spreading sycamores. Would he ever see them again, he wondered? Would he ever see any of it again?

As soon as the thought occurred to him, he quickly suppressed it for fear that he might cry. Instead, he tried to focus on Grandpa's earlier description of him. Blue or not, he reminded himself firmly, he was still a space explorer. A *brave* space explorer. He wasn't a cry-baby.

At last, his gaze returned to the lunar landscape. The Ocean of Storms seemed to go on forever. It was an expanse of dark rock, broken only by occasional "islands" of lighter rock. He wanted to look at them, but whenever he tried they were already out of sight.

He turned to the others.

"Does anyone *live* here?" he asked. "On the moon, I mean?"

Headlice was stroking Waldo on the green sofa. Every time she raised her hand, he tried to escape. She was either oblivious to this or else didn't care, because whenever he rose from the cushion, she simply petted him firmly back into position.

"No idea!" she said brightly.

"Well I know *you* don't know," he said grumpily. "I thought Grandpa might."

The man in question was at the console with a plastic ruler, trying to measure something on the screen. He seemed a bit harassed.

"Might know what?" he wondered wearily.

"Whether anyone lives on the moon," said Bradley. "I don't mean at Moon House. I mean—I mean out in the wild."

"Yes, of course—but what do you mean, the moon? *Which* moon?"

"The actual moon," said Bradley. "You know. *The moon.*"

Grandpa shot him a withering look.

"I know what you meant. I was trying to make a point! There are *hundreds* of moons in the Solar System, Bradley. Typical Earthling arrogance to name yours simply The Moon!"

Bradley thought that Grandpa was being a bit harsh, since he hadn't been involved in picking the name himself. Still, he wasn't in the mood for an argument.

"Well all right," he said. "What else is it called?"

Grandpa opened his mouth to reply, then realised—in a moment of visible panic—that he didn't actually know.

"But it *is* called something," he insisted—"and

if you wait right there, I'll tell you what."

He floated to the cupboard and came back with an enormous encyclopaedia. It was covered in bright blue fur—the pelt of some exotic alien—which obscured his hands entirely when he opened it at the index.

"Right," he said. "Give me a second."

After a while, he tutted, shut the book, and took it back to the cupboard in a huff. He went to the console and picked up his ruler.

"Turns out it's just called the moon," he admitted eventually.

"Fine—but does anyone *live* here?" asked Bradley again.

"What?—oh—yes—the lunatics!"

Bradley was filled with a sudden desire to show off how clever he was.

"They're called *lunatics* because they live on the moon," he explained to Headlice. "It comes from the word *lunar.* They used to think that the moon could drive you mad, so if you went insane, they called you a lunatic. But that's not what Grandpa meant."

"It's *exactly* what I meant," corrected Grandpa from the console. "Look around you. It's a dump! The *Selenites* must be nuts to stick it out here. Maybe that's why I get along with them so well. They're as crazy as I am. I used to come here quite a lot when I lived on Earth, you know. It was my secret getaway."

Bradley returned to the porthole, seeing if he could spot any evidence of them.

"What do they do down there?" he wondered.

"They mine helium-3," said Grandpa. "Use it for fuel. They're an extraordinarily private race, you know. Spend half their time in helium-powered invisibility suits. That's why your Earth scientists don't know about them. They let me borrow one of their suits, a long time ago, in return for a crate of Gee Whiz Soda."

It wasn't long before they reached what Grandpa called *the coastline*. Ghostly white cliffs rose from the dark plain, and for a second, the Ocean of Storms looked like a real ocean. High on a clifftop, surrounded by stars, was Moon House: an enormous stately home with round turrets, all encased in a clear glass bubble. The whole complex was concealed by some kind of invisibility field, and only swam into view when they came within range.

"Are you ready to check in?" asked Grandpa.

"I guess so," said Bradley.

He watched Moon House as they circled it. The bright windows beckoned them closer, and Grandpa took them down.

The interior was very mundane, and the gravity was set to one gee—making it very similar to Earth. It wasn't in the least bit exotic. Apart from the view from the windows, it could have been an old school building anywhere in England. The reception had a wooden counter with a bell, and Grandpa—being his usual forthright self—marched right up to it and started pressing it noisily.

"Hello?" he called.

They expected a receptionist to emerge from the back room. Instead, a smiling doctor came from one of the corridors. He looked exactly like a human, except for the fact that his beard and moustache were metallic purple.

"Welcome to Moon House!" he said warmly. "I'm Dr Quarg. Which one of you is poorly?"

"That one," said Grandpa—jerking a thumb at Bradley. "The one who's gone blue."

The doctor leaned forward to inspect Bradley. He stared into both of his eyes, then made him say *"Ah..."* so he could shine a torch into his mouth.

"Good grief," he said—stroking his purple whiskers. "You really *are* poorly, aren't you? Well! I intend to put you on a course of cheesecake and chocolate pudding! How does that sound?"

Bradley was surprised.

"It sounds great!" he said.

Before he could be led away, a second doctor came storming out of the corridor. He was about seven feet tall, but much of his height came from a towering forehead. His eyebrows grew unevenly up it like creeping ivy, eventually joining the hair at the very top of it.

"*There* you are, Mr Queegleplax!" he said—talking to the one who had called himself Dr Quarg. "You've missed your last three treatments! You *know* what happens when you don't take your medicine!"

"But I'm Dr Quarg," protested the imposter. "Dr Jonathan Quarg. I've got a PhD!"

The doctor tried to manhandle him away.

"Come on, Mr Queegleplax! What will you decide to be next? A fireman? A farmer? *Where* did you find that doctor's outfit? And *where* did you find purple hair dye, of all things? Come on. Let's get you back to your room and see if we can wash it off."

Having said which, he turned to Bradley.

"I'm Dr Eris," he explained. "Sorry about that! I'll be back in a second to show you to your room. Based on your appearance, I'd recommend a course of *sonic treatments.* We may be able to hasten your recovery by reversing the polarity of the—hang on—I'll be back in a minute."

Before he could usher the escapee away, a third doctor came out of the corridor. His head was like a ripe red plum, and his eyes rose from the top of it on long stalks. He looked very harassed and was holding a clipboard in each hand. When he saw who was in reception, his face lit up.

"Ah! *There* you are!" he said. "Mr Queegleplax and Mr Zorgon, at it again!"

"But I'm Dr Eris," said Mr Zorgon—still holding his captive.

"And I'm Dr Quarg," protested the other. "Dr Jonathan Quarg—PhD!"

The doctor was unimpressed.

"*Neither* of you are doctors," he said firmly. "We've been through this before. Now come on. Are you going to return to your rooms, or must I get the orderlies to sedate you?"

Then he turned to Bradley and looked him up and down.

"You look like you've been treated for space malaria," he said with authority. "I presume you're here to get over it?"

Bradley nodded.

"Good," said the doctor. "My name is Dr Hizzle, and I'm going to treat you with a course of magic and moonbeams! Tee hee!"

At last, the receptionist came out of the back room. When she saw the three men dressed as doctors, she looked startled and pressed a silent alarm under the counter. Moments later, burly alien orderlies entered from all directions.

Headlice nudged Bradley.

"This is hilarious!" she said excitedly.

The orderlies grabbed the three imposters and restrained them. At last, a fourth doctor came into the reception. He was the most alien-looking out of all of them. He floated three feet above the ground and had no arms or legs—or even much of a body, for that matter. His scarlet head was enormous and throbbed in consternation.

Bradley looked at the receptionist in alarm.

"Don't worry," she called over her desk. "That's the real one!"

At first, the floating doctor didn't pay them

much attention. He was too busy supervising the restraint of the three imposters.

"Sedate them if you have to!" he said gruffly. "I'm sick of this lot. I see they've got doctors' uniforms again. Are we not locking that cupboard any more?"

At last, he turned to Grandpa, Bradley and Headlice.

"Very sad," he said, shaking his head. "They're suffering from *coordinated doctor impersonation disorder.* It's funny the first time, but it soon gets old. Who's the patient here?"

"Me," said Bradley. "I'm Bradley."

"Space malaria, I presume?"

"That's right," said Bradley. "Space malaria. So what are you going to prescribe me? Fizzy pop and peaches?"

"Ha ha! Well—nothing," admitted the doctor. "You've had all the treatment you need. We'll just provide you with an environment to recover—and help you, if we can, to come to terms with the side effects of your previous treatment."

Bradley looked at his indigo hands and sighed.

"Won't be easy," he admitted.

"I know," said the doctor gently. "I'm Dr Oberon, by the way. Would you like to see your room?"

"*Three* rooms," corrected Grandpa.

He'd been leaning on the counter, chatting up the receptionist, but turned around at the mention of a room.

"I think we could *all* do with a bit of 'R' and 'R'!" he said brightly. "Especially after all those parties on Mercury. Why—I don't know about you, Headlice, but I feel like we haven't stopped since the Asteroid Belt!"

Dr Oberon wasn't impressed.

"Sorry," he said firmly. "One room and one room only. We have limited resources here. We're a charity—not a holiday camp! Bradley, you can say goodbye to them in a moment. They need to fill out some forms at the counter."

Bradley looked at the others and shrugged. Then he followed the floating doctor out of the reception and into the corridor, wondering what lay in store for him at Moon House.

CREAM OF COMET SOUP

DR OBERON LED the way down the long hall. In the gloom, his giant head—which was dark and red, like lava—seemed almost to glow like hot coals.

"Come along!" he said.

Bradley traipsed wearily after him. Now that he was no longer weightless, he was starting to feel quite weak and ill again. He envied how Dr Oberon could float ahead of him, as light and graceful as a hot air balloon.

"I'm sure your friends think I'm very rude," said the doctor matter-of-factly. "And I'm sorry to drag you away from them so abruptly. But I just wanted to ask you a couple of questions before we let them go. What are you doing in space?"

Bradley was surprised by his directness.

"What?   Oh—well it was meant to be a holiday," he explained.   "It turned out more like an adventure."

"But Earthlings don't normally holiday in space," said Dr Oberon pointedly.   "Certainly not young boys, and certainly not so far from home!   Who's the man looking after you?   I noticed a green tinge in the corners of his eyes. He looks like he's from Grabelon."

"He is.   He's my Grandpa."

Dr Oberon span in the air to face Bradley. His enormous red features seemed suddenly very serious.

"Earth is a protected nature reserve," he pointed out.   "You're not meant to visit without a special license—let alone start a family there! And technically, removing *you* from your natural environment probably counts as wildlife smuggling!   It sounds like your Grandpa has broken quite a few of our space laws."

Bradley bristled at being called *wildlife*.

"And I must say," continued the doctor,

looking him up and down—"it rather looks like you've been a victim of your Grandpa's poor judgement."

"What?!—no—it's been worth every second," said Bradley—surprised by how quickly the words sprang to his lips. "I'm not a child. I mean, obviously I *am* a child. But I'm not a victim. I'm a proper space explorer. Grandpa said so. And Dad's not even that angry about it. He had my pocket money sent out to me. Look."

Dr Oberon didn't look convinced when Bradley showed him the fifty pees.

"I've got half a mind to report your Grandpa to the authorities," he said darkly. "But maybe I won't. Come on. Let's see your room. I think you'll be pleased with the facilities. Our new patrons have been very generous."

Bradley followed him.

"Who are your new patrons?" he wondered.

"A society of rich philanthropists," replied Dr Oberon, "who call themselves *The Andromeda Club.* Have you heard of them?"

* * *

Bradley's blood ran cold. Of course he'd heard of the Andromeda Club. When they'd gone looking for treasure, the Andromeda Club had hired a gang of arachnid assassins to hunt them through space—hoping to find it first. Perhaps they hadn't heard that the treasure was a booby prize. Perhaps they still wanted it for themselves. Perhaps they were plotting to find them and punish them...

He didn't say this out loud, however. He just followed Dr Oberon down the corridor, until they came at last to an empty room.

As promised, the facilities at Moon House were very good. Bradley had a large room with a lunar view, an *en suite* bathroom, and a big comfy bed that could be raised or lowered with a button. There was a lamp on a bedside cabinet, and a little unit on the wall that could blow out hot or cold air on demand. All the furniture looked very familiar, as if it had been shipped specially from Earth.

"We can take your space suit in for a service," said Dr Oberon. "The self-cleaning unit probably needs a new filter by now. We have meals-on-wheels, a library, a gym—you name it. You'll be very comfortable here. Can you see that dial on the wall?"

Bradley nodded.

"That's the artificial gravity. Every room here has a dial just like it. You can make it higher or lower. In your case, I recommend you don't make it any lower. The space malaria has weakened you, and you need to build up your strength. In the communal areas, the gravity is always set to one gee."

Bradley looked around. The room was light and spacious. It was just what he needed. The only fly in the ointment was the fact that the Andromeda Club were somehow involved. That disquieting truth fell across the room like a shadow.

"Well?" said the doctor.

"It looks great," said Bradley.

Then the doctor took him to the reception to

say his goodbyes.

"We'll be back soon," promised Grandpa. "You stay put and get better. Toodle-pip!"

And that was that. Bradley stayed put—feeling, as he lay in bed with the meals-on-wheels menu, as lonely as he'd ever felt in his whole life.

Still—the menu looked pretty good. As a guest of the Andromeda Club, he got to choose from the best cuisine of the entire Solar System. He was about to tick the box for the full Grabelonian breakfast, since he'd had it before—and knew that he liked it—but then some of the other treats caught his eye.

Cream of comet soup. King-sized dolly mix. Cloudfish kebabs from the skies of Venus. Firecracker pudding, with glow-in-the-dark gravy from the Great Red Spot of Jupiter! Findus Crispy Pancakes™ from Planet Earth. The list went on and on.

"I wonder how many things I'm allowed to order?" he said out loud.

"As many as you want!" barked a voice from

above—making him jump. *"The Andromeda Club has twelve trained chefs, fresh from the kitchen of the Hale Bop Brasserie. They've sourced the* crème de la crème *of interplanetary cuisine and want you to enjoy as much of it as possible!"*

Bradley scanned the ceiling but couldn't see anyone. Eventually, he realised that there was a little speaker on the wall behind him.

"Can you understand me?" he asked.

"Of course!" said the voice from the speaker. *"I'm a computer program. Our patrons are very interested in artificial intelligence. In fact, they sponsor twelve different research programmes at nine different universities. I'm Helpotron, and I can be accessed from any room at Moon House. I'll understand anything you say to me."*

"Well fancy that," said Bradley.

"I will!" promised the voice.

"Okay—well how big is the dolly mix?"

"Error!" said the voice cheerily. *"Did you mean, how big are those jolly bricks?"*

Bradley was about to explain that he didn't, but then got curious and said that he did.

"*Error!*" said the voice. "*I'm afraid I don't know the answer to that question. Would you like to hear about the king-sized dolly mix?*"

"Yes!" said Bradley quickly. "I'd like to know how big it is."

"*Moon House is the biggest care facility on this side of the Asteroid Belt. Would you like to hear some relaxing music?*"

"I would, actually," said Bradley.

"*Me too,*" said Helpotron sadly. And then he fell silent.

After a while, a nurse collected Bradley's order, and then another one came with a trolley. Bradley couldn't believe how big the dolly mix was. If you've never had dolly mix before—because they might not make it where you come from—then I'd better explain what it is. It's a kind of sweet that comes in a bag. You get an assortment of fondant cubes, sugary cylinders, and sparkling fruit jellies. Normally, each is about the size of your fingertip.

The king-sized dolly mix, on the other hand, was truly enormous. There were only three pieces, but Bradley wasn't sure he could finish even two of them. On the left of the tray was a square yellow one, almost as large as a Rubik's Cube. On the right was a cylinder of green and white fondant, thicker than Bradley's wrist. And in the centre was an enormous sparkling jelly, redder than Mars, rising like the summit of Olympus Mons.

He couldn't believe his eyes. Normally, with dolly mix, you might throw a whole handful in your mouth, or squish two together to make an entirely new one. But in Moon House, the sweets were so big that they came with a knife and fork.

He cut into the yellow cube, revealing the sweet white interior.

"Brilliant!" he said greedily. And then he got stuck in.

Half an hour later, Dr Oberon came to check on him.

"What's wrong with you?" he wondered in surprise.

Bradley was lying on his back with his hand over his eyes.

"I've eaten too many sweets," he said bleakly. "I had the king-sized dolly mix!"

Dr Oberon looked at him in contempt.

"*King-sized dolly mix?* Come on, Bradley! That's hardly a suitable meal for an Earthling! We cater for all kinds of lifeforms here. Why didn't you have the Findus Crispy Pancakes?"

"I don't know!" cried Bradley in despair.

The doctor had little sympathy.

"So do I have to choose your meals for you," he threatened, "or will you pick something more appropriate next time?"

"I'll pick something more appropriate next time," said Bradley unhappily.

The doctor floated to the head of the bed.

"Perhaps *Helpotron* can advise you," he suggested. "Helpotron! Would you please tell Bradley which of our meals are suitable for Earthlings?"

"*Error!*" said Helpotron. "*Did you mean, which of our seals is cuter than a gosling?*"

Dr Oberon tried to hide his annoyance.

"No," he said slowly. "I did not. I want you tell us what *meals* are suitable for *Earthlings.*"

Helpotron paused to think about it.

"King-sized dolly mix?" he said eventually.

Dr Oberon's face glowed darkly.

"King-sized dolly mix," he said quietly, "is *not* suitable for Earthlings."

"Not true!" countered Helpotron. *"One-hundred percent of our Earthling guests ordered king-sized dolly mix."*

"That's because Bradley is our first ever Earthling guest," explained the doctor patiently, "and he made a mistake. Didn't you, Bradley?"

"People who enjoyed king-sized dolly mix also enjoyed cream of comet soup," continued Helpotron, ignoring this information. *"Would you like some cream of comet soup, Bradley?"*

Bradley had recovered a bit by this point.

"I would!" he said eagerly.

Dr Oberon silenced him with a glare.

"Cream of comet soup," he pointed out, "contains nothing of nutritional value for a human. I take it you're feeling better?"

Bradley shrugged.

"A bit," he admitted.

"Right," said Dr Oberon. "In that case, you can get out of bed. I'll show you the rest of the South Wing."

And he floated off, leaving Bradley to follow.

THE RICHEST MAN ON MARS

BRADLEY GREW CURIOUS as they walked back up the corridor. Previously, he hadn't paid his surroundings much attention. Now he was struck by them. The walls had dark wooden panelling, like a stately home on planet Earth. He ran a finger along it, enjoying the familiar feel of the wood's grain. Every now and then, he had to lift his finger from the wall to avoid a picture frame.

The pictures themselves were images from Earth. One showed a red double-decker bus passing Nelson's Column. Another showed the Statue of Liberty, raising her torch over New York harbour. Then there were smiling faces at a Rio carnival. The Great Pyramid at Giza. The crossed swords of Baghdad. A whale's tail, rising up to slap the waves like a giant carpet-beater...

"Why is everything so *Earth-like* here?" wondered Bradley out loud.

"Well it wasn't *my* choice to do it like this," replied Dr Oberon—"I think it's tacky—but it's the kind of thing our guests want to see. It's a novelty to be so close to Earth. I suppose you think that's silly."

"Not really," said Bradley. "It's comforting. Exactly what I need!"

They paused at an enormous pair of double doors.

"This is the Andromeda Ballroom," said Dr Oberon—indicating that Bradley should look inside. "It's a bit swish, isn't it? Our patrons paid for it. They're hosting an event here soon, in fact. The Star of Galatea will be on display. Have you heard of it? It's a thousand carat diamond, brighter and bluer than the seas of Neptune. A thousand carats! It must be bigger than a football."

Bradley held the door open a crack. The

Andromeda Ballroom certainly *was* a bit swish—but there was something about it that made him uneasy. The tables and chairs were as dark as dark chocolate. The soft furnishings were the colour of black cherries. Through the large windows, there was nothing to see except a dark starry sky, and the glowing white craters of the moon.

"Nice," he said.

In the middle of the room was a round stage with a microphone stand. Directly over it was an enormous chandelier, ten feet across, with a thousand trembling shards of dark crystal. It was supported by a rubber-coated cable, no thicker than Bradley's finger. This had been pulled so taut by the weight of the chandelier that (he imagined) it would sound a deep note if he plucked it, like the bottom string of a bass guitar.

He turned to Dr Oberon.

"I wouldn't want to stand under that chandelier," he told him. "The cable doesn't look strong enough!"

"Quite!" agreed Dr Oberon gravely. "I made the same observation when they put it up. Apparently, it's not heavy enough to break the cable—but I wouldn't like to stand under it, all the same!"

He scanned the interior and pulled an unhappy face.

"In fact, I don't like to be in the Andromeda Ballroom at all," he admitted. "It doesn't feel right. Moon House is meant to be a place of healing—not of opulence! But our patrons have funded plenty of good work here, so I mustn't grumble at this—ah—little *indulgence* of theirs."

Finally, they came to the common room. It had comfy chairs, card tables, and lush green plants in terracotta pots. At first, these looked like plants from Earth—but then one rustled, and a pair of eyes emerged to inspect the newcomers. When Bradley took a closer look, he realised that the eyes belonged to the plant itself, rather than a creature hiding in the foliage.

Before long, he found his gaze drawn to the

far end of the room. It had been made larger by adding a glass conservatory, which was surrounded on all sides by lunar desert. Outside, under the supervision of a nurse, someone was bouncing lightly on the spot, testing his legs in the lower moon gravity. He looked like he was underwater. The nurse encouraged him to try jumping higher and higher, until he was rocketing skyward in slow motion. Behind him, barely visible, was a distorted image of Moon House, reflected on the inside of the bubble that enclosed the grounds. Behind *that,* like a big blue marble swirled with white, was planet Earth against a starry sky.

As Bradley gazed at it, something moved in his peripheral vision, and he realised that someone was sitting in the conservatory.

"Nurse!" demanded the elderly man. "Nurse!"

He'd been hiding behind an enormous newspaper—a broadsheet called the *Times of Mars*—which was covered with dense indigo print and silver holograms. Now, as he tried to catch the attention of a nurse, it lay on his knees like a blanket. He had a stony red face with a goatee, and a long cruel hook of a nose. His pyjamas were striped white and green, making him look like a giant tube of toothpaste.

"I would like a pot of tea," he told the nurse who went over. "Not Martian tea. *Jovian* tea. The kind you get on Jupiter. And bring me a bowl of sugar cubes, too."

The nurse went pale with fright.

"Sugar? Are you sure, sir? Wouldn't you rather have it plain?"

"I will have it with sugar."

"But sugar makes Jovian tea *explode*," protested the nurse in a small voice.

"Explode?" said the man with scorn. "I assure you, I know exactly what I'm doing with the sugar. You can get one in quite safely, and a second if you stir it slowly. I know for a fact that a master tea-maker can add a third without fear. I learned the knack from the tea shops of Europa. You needn't worry."

Bradley watched the nurse leave, then turned

to Dr Oberon.

"Who's that?" he asked him.

"That's one of our billionaire patrons," explained the doctor. "Lord Victor Bonneville. He recently took up residence here. He says he's getting old and infirm, but between you and me, he's as fit as a fiddle! I think he likes to keep an eye on how the club funds are being spent."

As he spoke, the nurse went scurrying back to the conservatory with a teapot on a tray. Next to it was a bowl of sparkling sugar cubes.

"Here you go," he said nervously.

Lord Victor poured out the silvery tea, looked at him pointedly, and then—with an air of supreme confidence—held a single white cube over the teacup. The instant he let it fall, the cup exploded with a terrifying *BANG!*

All around the room, fragments of the cup struck various surfaces, making diverse sound effects. A wooden thud here—a glassy tinkle there—a sound like a marble being dropped on a glass table. Not far from Bradley, a leaf fell from one of the plants, snipped neatly from its stem by a china fragment. Closer to the site of the explosion, tea had sprayed the sugar bowl, making it fizz dangerously.

All heads turned to Lord Victor, who merely smiled humourlessly. He picked up his paper and tried to soak up the spillage.

"I seem to have lost the knack," he conceded. "But never mind. Fetch me a new teacup," he told the cowering nurse, "and I'll try it *without* the sugar for now."

Watching from the doorway, Bradley didn't know what to make of Lord Victor. The billionaire's features were cold and hard, but not unkind. He looked like the kind of person who didn't suffer fools gladly, but wouldn't have the heart to torment one.

"How did he get so rich?" wondered Bradley.

"Through water," said Dr Oberon. "Since the canals dried up, the water on Mars is mined from the ice caps. They couldn't mine at the South Pole because it was full of deadly giant centipedes. Lord Victor conquered it and made

71

billions mining the water there. He's the richest man on Mars."

"And he's in the Andromeda Club?"

"Of course," said Dr Oberon. "You should hear his stories about the clubhouse casino!"

Bradley had seen the clubhouse during a visit to Grabelon, which was the planet where Grandpa had been born and raised. The entrance to the club had a plush red carpet, and a door so dark not even light seemed to escape from it.

"Well I'm sure he won't want us gawping at him," said Bradley at last. "Is that the end of my tour?"

"For now," said Dr Oberon. "I bet you want chance to explore. Do stick to the South Wing though. Nowadays, our patrons use the North Wing for private research projects. It's all very hush-hush. *I'm* not even allowed to see what goes on in there—let alone you!"

And with those thought-provoking words, he floated from the common room, leaving Bradley to his own devices.

A DOUBLE DOSE OF SPACE MEASLES

AT FIRST, BRADLEY hovered by the entrance to the common room. He wondered whether he should introduce himself to someone, or join a game of dominoes, but his heart sank at the thought of it. All the other guests looked so *old.*

He was going to wander back to his room, but then curiosity got the better of him. Despite Dr Oberon's warning, he cut across the empty reception to look at the mysterious North Wing. It hadn't been pointed out to him, but he guessed that it would be the corridor opposite the South Wing, which Dr Oberon had just shown him.

He wouldn't go *too* far inside, he decided. It was too dangerous, given that the Andromeda Club had something to do with it. But at the end of the day, he was a space explorer now— not an invalid! Grandpa would positively *expect* him to have a sniff around, and he felt buoyed by the thought of meeting that expectation. If he got caught, he could always pretend that he'd been confused about where the North Wing started.

A shiver of excitement raced up his spine. Grandpa would be proud of him—that was for sure. This was his chance to justify the glowing report that had been given to Dad.

He stopped at the entrance to the corridor, wondering how far he was prepared to take his solo investigation.

"Hello?" he called into the darkness.

He looked furtively over his shoulder, then stepped inside. The minute he did, he felt very strongly that he wasn't meant to be there. The walls were painted with cheap white emulsion, as if the public weren't meant to see them. The lights were much too far apart, letting darkness pool at regular intervals.

"Hello?" he said again. "Is anyone here?"

The corridor had no doors and led only to a distant junction. He set off towards it, then stopped very quickly. For some reason he couldn't quite put his finger on, the long gloomy corridor filled him with dread.

Suddenly, he noticed a speaker embedded in the wall. It was exactly like the one above his bed.

"Helpotron!" he whispered. "Are you there?"

There was a pregnant pause.

"*Error!*" whispered the speaker after a while. "*Did you mean, am I a bear?*"

Bradley ignored the ridiculous question.

"Did you know that I was here?"

"*Of course I did. I know the location of every guest to within a metre.*"

"What's at the end of this corridor?"

"*I'm not allowed to say. Why are you whispering?*"

"Because I'm not meant to be here! Why are

you whispering?"

"*I'm just a bit creeped out.*"

"Why? What happens in the North Wing?"

"*Error!*" said Helpotron. "*Did you mean—*"

"Oh, give over," said Bradley. "Don't pretend. I know you understood me. What are the Andromeda Club doing here?"

No answer was returned—and the longer he stood there waiting, the less happy he felt. Hairs were beginning to rise on the back of his neck, and he had to fight an irrational urge to flee.

"Helpotron!" he said firmly—but he could detect a note of panic in his own voice.

With every second, the panic grew. Soon, his head was almost swimming with fear.

He made a snap judgement. Or rather, his legs made it for him.

"Never mind," he said abruptly.

He panicked and ran back to reception, then slowed down and walked sheepishly to his room.

* * *

He spent the rest of the day in a funk. So much for being a brave space explorer! He lay on his bed, stewing over how he'd fled from the corridor—scurrying away with his tail between his legs.

It was frustrating because he'd actually done some very dangerous things since leaving Earth. He'd gone face to face with that pirate, who had the ugly scar and those grasping grey hands. He'd also faced arachnid assassins—more than once!—and a homicidal giant robot.

It seemed only natural for him to investigate the North Wing. It was exactly what Grandpa would have done in his position. So why had he chickened out?

His heart sank. The answer was simple. Regardless of Grandpa's high opinion, at the end of the day, he was just a chicken. He hadn't even managed to ask Grandpa about bringing his mum back to life. He'd choked then, and he'd choked again at the entrance to the North Wing.

He could only conclude that none of his

experiences had actually made him any braver. Had they changed him at all, he wondered? Or were they things that had simply happened to him, in the way that raindrops happen to a rooftop?

He held up his blueberry-coloured hands, reminding himself of the one way that he actually *had* changed. On the outside at least, he was a transformed person. But beneath the navy blue hair and indigo skin, he was just boring old Bradley from planet Earth.

And with that miserable thought going round in his head—like a sad old sock in the washing machine of his mind—he fell fast asleep.

The next morning, he was roused by a nurse.

"You might want to go to reception," she said. "A few of your friends are there."

He frowned and rubbed his eyes.

"Isn't it a bit early for a visit?" he wondered.

"Well yes—but it's not a visit. They're actually checking in. They got ill overnight."

After she left, he hurried to the bathroom and

used the strange-looking urinal. It was like no urinal he'd ever seen before, and he had to stand on tiptoe. When he was done, he tried to operate the futuristic sink. There was only one tap, and it pointed directly upwards. He turned it on very carefully and was surprised when shaving foam began to gurgle out of it.

He turned it off and looked around in despair. Luckily, there was a speaker on the ceiling.

"Helpotron!" he said. "Quickly! How do I wash my hands?"

"Let me check my records," said Helpotron.

There was a pause.

"Previous guests," he revealed at last, *"enjoyed washing their hands in our luxurious* en suite *facilities!"*

"I know," said Bradley impatiently. "That's what I'm trying to do. How *exactly* do I wash my hands?"

"Why don't you use the water in the sink?"

"I'm *at* the sink, Helpotron. There's no water in it."

"That's not the sink. That's the luxury shaving

station, with luxury scented shaving foam."

"Then what's the sink?"

"You did a wee in it."

There was an awkward pause.

"So where do I go to the toilet?" said Bradley at last.

Helpotron thought it over.

"Guests who enjoyed weeing in the sink," came the eventual response, *"also enjoyed weeing in the luxury shaving station!"*

Bradley ignored this advice and looked behind him. In the corner was something that looked like a large ceramic vase.

"Is *that* the toilet?" he asked—pointing it out.

"Yes," said Helpotron.

"Great. And can we change the water in the sink?"

"The water in the sink is automatically replaced after every wash!" said Helpotron brightly.

"But I *can't* wash in it," said Bradley testily, "because I got confused and did a wee in it!"

"Yes. Stalemate!" acknowledged Helpotron.

Bradley groaned and stamped his foot.

"Fine," he said. "I'll improvise."

He lathered his hands in shaving foam and wiped them on a towel. Then he ate some toothpaste.

"That'll have to do," he said. "I've got to go to reception."

When he got there, he was confused—but not surprised—to find Grandpa, Headlice and Waldo waiting for him. Grandpa and Headlice were grinning from ear to ear, with bright red dots all over their faces. They looked like they'd been drawn on with a chunky felt-tipped pen. In addition to this striking symptom, Headlice was standing with her legs bent, like a cowboy.

"They're letting us check in this time," she said smugly. "Because we've been ill, you know."

"Yes," said Grandpa—smirking at the success of the ruse. "*Very* ill—the pair of us!"

"We're not making it up," added Headlice. "Honestly!"

"I was so ill it's a miracle I didn't die," claimed Grandpa.

"Well *I've* been at death's door," said Headlice—and then the pair of them burst out laughing.

Bradley wasn't convinced.

"Why? What's wrong?" he asked.

"Headlice is getting over space measles," explained Grandpa, with a wink, "and I've had glandular fever."

Headlice stopped smiling.

"Wait—*that's* not right," she said. "*You've* got space measles. I thought I had rickets?"

Grandpa looked blank.

"Rickets? Then why have you drawn spots on your face?"

"I haven't," said Headlice. "*You've* drawn spots on your face. I'm just standing with my legs a bit bent."

"What on Mars do you mean? I haven't drawn a single spot anywhere!"

"Well neither have I," said Headlice.

She shook her head in exasperation. Then she turned to Bradley.

"Is there a mirror nearby?" she asked wearily.

After a while, a nurse came over, took their temperatures, and confirmed—to their genuine surprise—that they really had caught space measles.

"Is he checking in as well?" asked the nurse—indicating Waldo with his pen. "What's up with him?"

Other than the fact that he looked worried—which was his default expression—the star-pup was the very picture of health as he floated around reception. Grandpa studied him, wondering what to say. Then he smiled, clicked his fingers, and span to face the nurse.

"A recovering alcoholic!" he assured him.

The nurse rolled his eyes.

"Fine! The star-pup can stay. He won't need a room of his own, will he?"

"He can stay with me," said Bradley quickly. "He's my pet."

"And what a fine job you've done looking after him!" said the nurse—writing *recovering alcoholic* in large letters on a clipboard. "Anything else?"

"Yes," said Bradley firmly. "There's a problem with my sink. It needs new water."

"Okay," said the nurse. "We can do that. No problem. And as for you two," he added, turning to the newcomers, "we'll get you settled in shortly. Dr Oberon is doing his rounds just now, but I'm sure he'll give you a tour later."

Grandpa picked up a newspaper and sat down with it.

"No rush," he said.

And he pulled out a pen and started the crossword.

While Grandpa got on with his puzzle, Headlice turned her attention to Bradley. He was touched—and slightly alarmed—by how pleased she was to see him. Before he could jump out of reach, she linked arms with him and escorted him aimlessly around, telling him what she'd been up to.

After a while, Bradley got bored of listening and started to tune her out. It was strangely relaxing, letting himself get marched around without paying attention to what she was actually saying. Soon, his eyes began to wander as well. The receptionist was putting up a poster, which showed a brilliant blue gem on a white plinth. It was an advert for the Star of Galatea—the thousand carat diamond, which was due to be presented in the Andromeda Ballroom.

"Are you listening?" said Headlice suddenly.

"Mm? Oh—sorry—I was distracted for a moment. Look at that poster."

"It's lovely! What is it?"

"The Star of Galatea," he told her. "It's a massive diamond. They're going to have some kind of ball to celebrate it being here. I don't know whether we'll be invited or not."

"Well I hope we are!" said Headlice. "It looks gorgeous!"

In the days that followed, Bradley found it energising to be back with his friends. Space measles was a mild condition, and other than the spots, their main symptoms seemed to be sleepiness, lack of appetite, and (according to

Grandpa) a slight ache in the knees and elbows. They certainly weren't invalids, and sometimes, they would go to the gym or bounce around in the grounds of Moon House.

He agonised over whether he should tell them about the link to the Andromeda Club, but resolved against it in a moment of quiet self-loathing. He knew that Grandpa would want to investigate, and the thought of returning to the North Wing made him anxious and panicky.

He rationalised it away and tried not to think about it. After all, he was ill. No one could blame him (he reasoned) for taking a break from being a brave space explorer when he was actually ill.

And the truth is, chicken or not, he genuinely *was* still getting over his space malaria. Sometimes, he felt fine. Other days, he just wanted a bit of time to himself. When that happened, he would go to the common room and sit in the glass conservatory, surrounded by miles and miles of lunar desert.

There was something very peaceful about the

view from the conservatory. However, it wasn't long before Grandpa found him there and ruined it for him.

"Careful!" he told him. "While you're looking out, someone else might be looking in!"

Bradley wasn't convinced.

"There's nothing to see for miles and miles," he pointed out. "Where would they hide?"

Grandpa tapped his nose.

"Aha!" he said. "Remember what I told you about the *Selenites.* They have helium-powered invisibility suits. Why—there might be a whole gang of them right outside, watching you and making notes! I hope you've not been picking your nose, young man!"

After that, the conservatory lost its appeal for Bradley. Instead of feeling peaceful there, he felt exposed and paranoid. Worse, there were times when a strange depression came over him, and he couldn't even make it to the common room. On those occasions, he just lay in bed talking to Helpotron, and running his hands through Waldo's fur.

During those hours, his thoughts sometimes returned to the North Wing—but he never brought it up with Helpotron. Partly because it was hard to get any sense out of him, but mainly because even the thought of that corridor filled him with dread—and the fact that he didn't know why made it twice as troubling.

Mystery at Moon House!

It was Grandpa who solved the riddle of the scary corridor. They'd been in Moon House for some days and were wondering what to do over breakfast. Headlice finished her toast, then made the innocent suggestion that they could explore the North Wing for a change.

"The nurse told me I wasn't allowed to go down there," she explained. "So now I sort of want to."

Without thinking, Bradley snorted at the mere idea of it.

"No chance!" he told her. "You won't get me anywhere near that place!"

Grandpa stopped eating and looked at him quizzically.

"Won't we? Why not?" he wondered.

Bradley looked surprised, then scowled and made to leave. Then he sat back down, defeated.

At last, he buried his head in his hands and confessed everything.

"There's something I haven't told you," he said. "It's about Moon House. The whole thing is paid for by the Andromeda Club."

Grandpa looked surprised.

"What—*the* Andromeda Club? The one that paid arachnid assassins to hunt us down?"

Bradley nodded.

"The North Wing is off-limits because they use it for private research projects," he explained. "Not even Dr Oberon knows what's down there. I tried to investigate it by myself, because I thought that's what you'd want. But the minute I set foot in there, I started to panic. Eventually I just ran off. Since then I've been trying to forget about it."

He expected Grandpa to look at him with contempt. Instead, the old astronaut seemed surprised and then thoughtful as he chewed a mouthful of sugary cereal.

"Well they *might* have installed a Discourager," he reasoned. "That would certainly explain why you took flight."

"What's a Discourager?" wondered Headlice.

He gestured for her to be patient while he swallowed.

"It does exactly what it says on the tin," he said at last. "It *discourages* people. It projects fear into the minds of nearby intruders. It's a kind of—I don't know if this will mean anything to you—a kind of shortwave psychostimulator. It runs off a three-pin quadripole battery and is about the size of a personal stereo."

"Personal stereo? You're talking in futuristic gobbledegook," complained Bradley.

Grandpa rolled his eyes.

"It doesn't matter. The point is, if you don't get out of range, it gets more and more intense until you do. In a sense, it's more effective than a locked door. When people see a locked door, they wonder what's behind it. With a

Discourager, they don't want to know. That's the difference."

Bradley paused to consider this information, then realised he was delighted by it.

"Of course!" he said. "It makes perfect sense! I'm *not* a chicken after all!"

Grandpa held up his hands.

"Now hang on," he warned. "It's just a theory. It could be that you just got spooked. But you shouldn't be so hard on yourself. You've been very ill."

He returned to his cereal.

"Anyway—let me finish my breakfast," he suggested, "and we'll check it out together."

As soon as the reception was empty, they went and stood in the entrance to the North Wing.

Bradley hovered at the mouth of the corridor, gripped by the same inexplicable dread. Headlice must have felt it too, because she let out a small gasp.

Grandpa seemed totally unaffected. He walked ten paces into the corridor, turned, and nodded.

"There's *definitely* a Discourager here," he told them. "One at least. Someone has something to hide!"

Bradley stayed where he was.

"But how do you know?" he wondered in a small voice.

"I know because I'm scared as well," said Grandpa. "I don't scare easily, so that in itself is suspicious. Something's putting it in my head."

"But if you're scared, then why have you walked halfway down the corridor?"

"Because I know it isn't real," said Grandpa, "which takes the bite out of it. And it's whetted my appetite for mystery. Come on in—before someone sees us!"

Bradley wasn't sure he could follow. He didn't even like to see someone else standing there. The old man looked very vulnerable. Bradley felt a prickly unease, as if—at any moment—clawing hands could burst from the walls or floor to seize his smiling Grandpa.

Then the focus of the fear shifted, and he was

no longer scared *for* Grandpa, but *of* him.

In the low light, the old man's face began to seem very alien. Even his moustache seemed weird and unnatural. In fact, with each passing second, the man in the corridor seemed less like Grandpa, and more like a malevolent being who just happened to look like him.

"Hurry up!" he urged. "The intensity is increasing. It'll get worse and worse until we get out of range."

Headlice nudged Bradley.

"Do you want to hold hands and go in together?" she offered kindly.

He scowled and turned red.

"I certainly do *not* want to hold hands and go in together!" he said hotly.

It wasn't long before they were spurred into action. Someone stirred in the little room behind the receptionist's desk. Bradley and Headlice shared a brief look, then entered the North Wing to avoid detection.

"Good," said Grandpa—taking each by a wrist. "Keep going. It can't hurt you. It's all in the mind. Trust me!"

Bradley's head swam and his heart raced. He felt like the walls were closing in on him. Grandpa powered ahead, pulling them deeper and deeper into the North Wing. His eyes were fixed on the far end of the corridor, so all Bradley could see was the back of his head. He half-expected him to whirl around, revealing his face to be that of an awful monster.

Then, very abruptly, the fear vanished. The three of them slowed to a surprised halt. Bradley looked around in bewilderment, taking in how mundane everything seemed. It was like a moment of revelation. Suddenly, he could see that the entrance to the North Wing was just a normal corridor with bad lighting.

"What happened?" he wondered.

"We've passed out of range," explained Grandpa. "Discouragers don't cover much ground. I guess they must be hidden in the ceiling near the entrance to the corridor."

Bradley was amazed. To test this explanation, he tried to walk back the way they'd come from.

Before he'd taken a couple of steps, the sight of the brightly lit reception filled him with genuine dread, and he desperately didn't want to go there.

He slowed to a halt, marvelling at how effective the Discouragers were. Even though he'd been to reception countless times—had just come from there, in fact—the thought of going there now made his skin crawl. But at the same time, he was learning to recognise that the fear wasn't real. It really did take the bite out of it.

Grandpa looked visibly pleased with himself.

"Well, I was right!" he said. "So now that we're here... who wants to explore?"

They went quietly down the corridor. Very quickly, they came to the junction at the end of it. Before they could consider which way to turn, they heard footsteps coming from round the corner.

"Leg it!" hissed Grandpa.

They beat a hasty retreat. As they did, the receptionist emerged from her little back room—just in time to see them spilling from the North Wing corridor.

"What—what were you doing down there?!" she wondered in alarm. "Hasn't anyone told you it's private?"

Bradley thought fast.

"We literally just popped our heads in," he told her. "We were going to have a look around but—I don't know what happened. I guess we changed our minds."

Headlice nodded.

"It's just not very nice down there," she explained.

"We'll be happier in the South Wing," agreed Grandpa.

The receptionist seemed mollified. Bradley wondered if she knew about the Discouragers. In either case, she didn't pursue the matter. She simply returned to her work, leaving the gang to go to the common room.

Grandpa, especially, seemed energised by the brief adventure.

"Well well well!" he whispered—pulling out a

chair and sitting down. "Discouragers! And the Andromeda Club, too! I wonder what's down there? I tell you what, kids—it feels good to have a mystery on the go!"

Bradley glanced in the direction of the conservatory. A familiar figure was sitting there, frowning at something in his *Times of Mars*.

Suddenly, Bradley remembered something he'd forgotten to tell them.

"There's something else," he told Grandpa and Headlice in a low voice. "One of the club members is staying here, right now. Lord Something Bonneville. He's sitting in the conservatory. Don't look."

Grandpa was visibly amazed, but resisted the temptation to turn round.

"Lord *Victor* Bonneville? He's the richest man on Mars! He's as fit as a fiddle, as far as I know. I wonder why he's here?"

Then he laughed with delight.

"Blistering black holes!" he cried. "There's something going on here, or I'm not an astronaut! We need to get to the bottom of it. We need to explore the North Wing properly."

But Headlice groaned.

"How can we?" she pointed out. "It's just long corridors. There's nowhere to hide. If someone comes we'll have to run away."

They lapsed into silence, mulling over the problem.

At last, something occurred to Bradley.

"Those people you told me about," he reminded Grandpa. "The lunatics—what were they called?"

It took Grandpa a second to work out what he meant.

"You mean the Selenites," he said. "The moon-people."

Bradley nodded.

"You said they've got *helium-powered invisibility suits,*" he reminded him. "They let you borrow one once. Do you think they'd let you borrow three of them now?"

Grandpa thought it over. Then his eyes twinkled, and a smile appeared beneath his enormous white moustache.

"Well," he said—"there's only one way to find out—isn't there!"

A LUNAR EXPEDITION

DR OBERON DIDN'T bat an eyelid when Grandpa said they were checking out for the afternoon. If anything, he encouraged the idea.

"It's good for you to get out," he assured Bradley. "But a few hours at most. Does that sound fair?"

Bradley nodded. They'd told Dr Oberon that they wanted to visit the Sea of Tranquillity—the site of the moon landings—so he could see the flag that the astronauts had left there.

Of course, that wasn't true. They were going to visit the Selenites and barter for three invisibility suits.

"Don't overdo it," continued the doctor. "It would be a shame if you exhausted yourself and had to miss tomorrow's big event—wouldn't it?"

Bradley frowned.

"What big event?" he wondered.

The doctor looked surprised.

"Haven't you seen the poster? Our patrons are throwing a party for all the guests, tomorrow night in the Andromeda Ballroom. The high point will be the unveiling of the Star of Galatea. It's the giant diamond that I told you about. Everyone will have a chance to admire it at close range."

Bradley nodded.

"Yes, sorry—of course," he said. "The Star of Galatea. I *did* see the poster, but I never got round to reading it properly. Well if that's the plan, I'll take it easy today and see you tomorrow night!"

Very soon, the gang had cast off in the spaceship. They raced across the moon's surface while Grandpa manned the console, looking for evidence of life on the monitors.

It didn't take long to find it. After just a few minutes, Captain Nosegay woke up, bubbling furiously in his glass dome.

"*Invisible lifeforms detected nearby!*" he said robotically.

Grandpa was delighted.

"Bingo!" he cried—tapping one of the screens. "They're still there. Okay. Get your mask on, Bradley. Headlice—you can use one of the emergency space suits. I'll get it out in a moment."

Bradley looked alarmed as the spaceship slowed to a halt.

"My mask?" he said. "Why? Do I need it?"

"Well of course," said Grandpa. "There's no air on the moon, is there? You'll need it to breathe!"

He went into the back and returned with armfuls of kit. The emergency suit, which he'd brought out for Headlice, was a kind of big shapeless overall, with transparent plastic for the face. He also had three small canisters and an assortment of tubes.

Bradley's heart sank.

"I left my mask at Moon House," he confessed.

Grandpa looked at his grandson in disbelief. His own mask was perched right on top of his head—like a flat cap.

"You *left* it? Sweet rings of Saturn! Did you not think you'd *need* it? Hang on—let me see if there's another emergency space suit."

Luckily, there was. Bradley climbed into it, looking and feeling ridiculous. It was made of thick dirty material, and the inside of it stank. Headlice got into hers as well, laughing as she staggered around and tried to line her face up with the see-through bit.

Then Grandpa inspected the air hoses, finding two with the right kind of fitting at the end. Finally, he was able to connect two of the canisters to the shapeless suits.

"Right," he said. "You're good to go. I'll just tell them we're coming."

He went to the console, turned on a radio, and started twiddling a knob.

"*Pasha graal!*" he told the microphone. "*Gol pasha! Pasha, graal!*"

He glanced at Bradley and then Headlice,

trying to gauge how impressed they were by his language skills.

"Did you hear that?" he suddenly asked. "That's the old moon language, that is. I'm fluent. Selenites like it when you make an effort. *Pasha! Graal! Pasha!*"

At last, a distant voice was heard in the static.

"*Pasha soto?* This is Gobacca Lang of the Bushwah Tribe. Is that you, you old scoundrel?"

Grandpa laughed in delight.

"Gobacca! Gobacca Lang! Why—you're still here! I *hoped* it would be you! How did you know it was me?"

"No one speaks our language as badly as you. You're just blurting out random words. What are you doing here?"

Grandpa laughed and winked at Bradley.

"Random words? *Galal!* Well, we're here to do a trade. Need a few *gazooki.* A bit of the old *thon casa, mel araag.* Heh heh! *Bishy bishy,* you old dog? *Bishy casa?*"

"Yeah. That doesn't mean anything. Come on

down and we'll talk. In English."

Grandpa looked briefly annoyed. Then he lowered his mask, found an air hose that fitted the mouth piece, and connected the last of the three canisters.

"Let's go," he told Bradley and Headlice—huffing and puffing through the mask.

Dropping through the hatch was like falling into a plughole.

Bradley shot out of it, propelled by the escaping air, and landed on his knees in silvery dust. Headlice followed, falling over when she tried to stand in her oversized suit. Then came Grandpa, pulling a rope ladder through the hatch as he fell.

The last of the air was rushing out, making a fierce down-draught that blew moon dust in all directions. Bradley tried to put some distance between himself and the spaceship. Then he turned round and looked up at the hatch in the bottom of it. A faint film of light seemed to be stretched over the opening, like the skin of a bubble. Grandpa had once told him that the hatch had something called a *fluid control field,* which let the air out in a controlled way—rather than it all trying to escape at once. Still, it was blasting out pretty quickly, disturbing moon dust that might not have moved for billions of years.

At last, very abruptly, it stopped. All the air had left the cabin.

Bradley bounced lightly, feeling like one of the Apollo astronauts. Headlice crawled behind him in slow motion, trying to get her right leg into the corresponding leg of the suit. After a while, Grandpa gestured for them to follow him over the lip of a crater.

Bradley bounced obligingly after him, while Headlice half-fell, half-crawled in the same direction. The crater seemed totally deserted. Then Bradley noticed the faint shimmer of an invisibility field, which intensified as they drew near. There was something in the crater, all right, but it had been hidden from view.

Soon, they were close enough for the

Selenite's camp to appear out of thin air, as if by magic. Bradley could see that there were six small igloos and one giant one in the crater. As they approached, a masked face appeared at the entrance to the largest one, waving them closer.

The entrance was covered by a sort of slitted membrane. While the slit was held open, strange silvery vapour leaked from the interior. Bradley realised that it was probably air. He wanted to ask Grandpa about this, but before he opened his mouth, it dawned on him that sound wouldn't travel through a vacuum anyway.

By the time he returned his attention to the igloo, the slit had been allowed to close, trapping the precious air inside. The stranger who had waved them closer was nowhere to be seen. Grandpa went on ahead and beckoned for them to follow.

When they got there, Headlice was the first to go inside. She got down on hands and knees and wormed her head through the plastic sheet. Grandpa helped her along with a good shove, then grabbed her leg and fed her in manually.

That achieved, he climbed in behind her and reached out to pull Bradley in after him.

Bradley struggled to follow. The plastic was incredibly stiff—presumably to keep the air in—and his shapeless baggy suit made it hard to manoeuvre.

At last, he managed to worm his way inside. He lay on his stomach, feeling weak and dizzy. He'd almost forgotten how ill he'd been, and the effort of forcing his way inside had quite taken it out of him.

When he stood up, the igloo's interior wasn't what he'd expected. In fact, it wasn't really an igloo at all. It was the mere tip of an enormous structure, most of which was totally submerged. A spiral staircase had been mined from the rock and was lit at intervals by warm yellow safety lamps.

Waiting at the top of these stairs—removing the mask to mop his brow—was the stranger who had waved them over. His smooth face was a magical blue colour, with pink and yellow lights dancing under the skin.

"I'm Gobacca," he told them. "Gobacca Lang of the Bushwah Clan. I'm an old friend of *that* rascal there," he added—jerking a thumb at Grandpa.

The rascal in question slid his mask back and grinned.

"Old friends indeed!" he agreed. "I used to lie low here whenever I was in trouble with your Grandma. Ha ha! *Graal! Graal!*"

Headlice looked impressed. She'd freed her head from the enormous space suit and her hair was sticking out at all angles.

"What does *graal* mean?" she wondered.

"It means tee-shirt," said Gobacca bluntly. "He always says it. I think he's got it muddled with *garel*. Garel means hello. Welcome to our helium mine."

Bradley and Headlice struggled from their space suits, then followed Grandpa and Gobacca down the stairs—bouncing slowly in the low moon gravity. The environment seemed very strange to Bradley. Because the mine was full of air, they could breathe, but they barely weighed a thing. It was like being underwater and on land at the same time. Their host led the way, moving so gracefully that he barely seemed to touch the steps beneath him.

"Nearly there," he promised.

At last, the stairs brought them to a dimly-lit cavern, hewn from the silvery moon-rock. Countless dark tunnels ran off in all directions, making Bradley wonder how big the mine was. Although it was gloomy, the moon-people were plain to see, because their faces glowed all kinds of colours—like the lights on a Christmas tree. Some of them were tinkering with machines. Others were pushing them into dark tunnels, or pulling them back out with ropes.

The machines themselves were enormous, with thundering pistons, spinning wheels, sprockets, chains, and shuddering levers. As the visitors made their way down the stairs, one of the contraptions overheated, causing a whistle to sound a shrill alarm. The Selenites drew back in fear, and those that were closest dived face down and covered their heads.

Moments later, there was a terrifying BANG! The machine shot out a fountain of white hot sparks, which faded as they fell around the cowering miners. It rattled loudly and fired a second and third time. After that, one of the miners managed to get close enough to turn it off, earning a round of applause from the others.

Once the drama was over, a few of the Selenites came over to greet their guests, and Grandpa tried to greet them in return—without success. Whatever he said to them made them scratch their heads and confer among themselves. Eventually, one of them vanished down a tunnel and came back with an armful of tee-shirts, which he tried to present to the guests.

"Graal?" he said hopefully.

Grandpa was mortified, but eventually agreed to accept one of the tee-shirts, since it had a picture on the front that made him chuckle.

Then they got to business. Grandpa explained—in English—that he was hoping to borrow three invisibility suits.

Gobacca looked surprised.

"Three?   After you lost that other one? Why?"

"Well!" began Grandpa—and he revealed that they were staying at Moon House, and explained (in very general terms) the mystery of the North Wing.

When he mentioned Moon House, Gobacca's face darkened, and the lights beneath his skin turned to less cheery colours.

"Be careful!" he warned. "Something very *odd* is going on in Moon House. Our scouts have been keeping a close eye on it!"

Grandpa's eyes sparkled.

"Really?" he replied in a whisper.   "Why? What have they seen?"

Gobacca looked over his shoulder, then leaned in to impart some sensitive information.

"Not long ago," he told his friend, "a cargo ship landed when the guests were asleep. We don't know what the cargo was, but when they brought it out in a crate, twenty armed guards came with it. They followed it all the way into Moon House."

"Twenty armed guards?" said Grandpa. "Must be something valuable!"

"There's a diamond coming to Moon House," explained Bradley. "The Star of Galatea. Maybe it's here already?"

But Gobacca shook his head.

"You don't understand," he told him. "The guards were pointing their guns *at* the cargo. Not away from it. And it was much too big to be a diamond."

Bradley's heart sank.

"Then it must be something dangerous," he said. "But what?"

Gobacca shrugged.

"No idea," he said. "The crate had *Project Vortex* written on the side. Ever since the cargo arrived, strange spaceships have come and gone in the night. Expensive ships with blacked-out windows."

Grandpa was delighted.

"Project Vortex!" he said. "Curiouser and

curiouser! I wonder what it is?"

"Well whatever it is, we don't like it," said Gobacca bluntly. "The last thing we need is for someone to raise a big stink on the moon. If the Earthlings get wind of it, we'll have them back in droves. That's the last thing we need. They just stomp all over everything—sticking flags in it!"

"*I'm* an Earthling," said Bradley grumpily—but Gobacca looked at him in disbelief.

"You can't be," he pointed out. "You're the colour of a blueberry!"

Grandpa waved for them both to shush.

"Listen, Gobacca—this Project Vortex stuff—it's exactly what we want to investigate," he assured him. "Lend us three of your suits. I promise we'll get to the bottom of it."

Gobacca thought it over. Eventually, he made a signal to one of his colleagues, who nodded and vanished down a dark tunnel. Moments later, she returned with the suits thrown over her shoulder. They were made out of stretchy brown fabric, and attached to each were gas canisters, round gauges with quivering red needles, gleaming gears, pistons, goggles, and elaborate copper plumbing.

He took the suits from her and gave them to the guests.

"Here you go," he said sternly. "And remember—don't lose them!"

Grandpa promised that he wouldn't. Then they said their farewells and returned to the surface.

When they got back to the spaceship, they couldn't take their suits off straight away. They had to stand around waiting for the cabin to fill with air again. Once it was safe to do so, Grandpa took off his mask and explained how the suits actually worked.

"It's perfectly simple," he assured them. "You turn the first wheel anticlockwise to release the helium, and clockwise to stop it again. When the needle is in the green, you twist the second wheel to start the reaction and turn the suit invisible."

Headlice was inspecting hers. She turned the soft balaclava bit inside-out.

"What's the earpiece for?" she wondered.

"That's so we can hear each other," said Grandpa. "The suits make us silent as well as invisible, so without them, we wouldn't be able to talk amongst ourselves."

"Clever," said Bradley.

Before long they were back at Moon House. Before they left the spaceship, Grandpa fiddled with each of the three suits, making them vanish. It was fascinating to watch them transform because it happened so slowly. First, the brown material faded to a grainy grey. Then Bradley could see through it—first faintly, then clearly. Eventually, he wasn't sure whether he was seeing the suits at all, or just a faint after-image of them inside his own eyes.

"Okay," said Grandpa, passing them around. "We need to get these suits inside. Try not to make it obvious that you're carrying something!"

Bradley didn't know quite what to do with his.

It felt weird to be holding something that he couldn't see. In the end, he just had to look away from his hands—which made the experience slightly less bewildering—and trust his sense of touch.

Luckily, they got the suits through reception and to Grandpa's room without incident. That achieved, Grandpa shut the door and made them visible again.

"I don't like leaving them on," he explained. "That's how I lost the first one! They'll be invisible enough if I stick 'em in my wardrobe."

They agreed that it would be best to explore the North Wing after dark. Each took a solemn oath to meet in Grandpa's room at midnight, and agreed to rest in their rooms until then.

Unfortunately, when Bradley lay down, he couldn't get settled. He tossed and turned impatiently, hoping that he would be able to nap for a bit. Eventually, he went and sat in the common room to kill some time. When he did, he was surprised to see that Lord Victor—

who was sitting in the conservatory with his copy of the *Times of Mars*—was watching him intently.

The Martian billionaire waved him over.

"Do you know who I am?" he asked.

Bradley nodded.

"Good!" said Lord Victor. "And I know who *you* are. It took me a while to work it out because you've turned blue. Earthlings aren't normally blue, are they? But you *are* an Earthling. So sit down. I want to talk to you."

Bradley did as he was told.

"You're the Earth-boy who stole our treasure," said Lord Victor. "The long-lost treasure of Mercury. Aren't you?"

"What? No!" insisted Bradley. "We didn't steal it. I swear."

"But you *did* steal the treasure map. You stole it from our clubhouse. Didn't you?"

Bradley shook his head.

"Someone *gave* us the map," he explained. "I swear on my life, we didn't know it was stolen. And the treasure wasn't even proper treasure. It

119

was just an ice-making machine. It certainly wasn't worth chasing us across space for!"

Lord Victor looked surprised, then burst out laughing. His red features creased like old leather. Once he'd finished, he made a dismissive gesture with his hand.

"To be honest, I couldn't care less about the treasure," he said. "I just wanted to check it was you. So you can trust me not to turn you in. But I was curious to meet you. I've been fascinated by Earth for a long, long time. Mars is a desert world, you know, but yours—why!—it's covered with water. Imagine that. Half the world, covered in water. All of our fairy tales are set on Earth, you know. Tell me—is the blue whale real, or is it just a myth?"

Bradley was taken aback. Lord Victor's face had lit up with excitement. In fact, he was leaning right out of his armchair. He almost looked like a child.

"It's real," replied Bradley.

Lord Victor looked delighted and slapped his thigh.

"Good grief! It really is real! What a wonderful world you live in. Have you ridden one? Is that even possible?"

Bradley shook his head.

"I've never ridden a blue whale. I don't think anyone has."

Lord Victor looked briefly disappointed, then smiled his cold thin smile.

"But you *have* been into space," he said generously. "Not many Earthlings can say the same, and none have been as far as you. You've been all the way to the edge of the Solar System, haven't you? In your own way, young man, you're as remarkable as the blue whale. Remind me—what's your name?"

"Bradley."

"Well, Bradley! You're a little young now, but perhaps you'll join our club when you're older. An Earthling in the Andromeda Club! Fancy that, eh? That'd be one in the eye for the other clubs, I'm sure!"

"Me? But I'm not even rich!" protested Bradley, backing away.

Lord Victor just rolled his eyes.

"Neither was I, to begin with. I was just a lowly captain. But I *got* rich. I saw an opportunity and took it—like you did, Bradley— when you first left Earth. I faced peril, just like you have. I see greatness in you, young Bradley. You could be just like me."

He reached deep into his dressing gown pocket, pulled out a silver case, and opened it. It was filled with blue cigarettes.

"Did you know," he began—putting one in his mouth—"that it was me who conquered the South Pole of Mars?"

Bradley nodded.

"The whole place was infested with giant centipedes," explained Lord Victor—going back to his pocket for a lighter. "Incredible creatures, those centipedes. A proud warrior race. When they reared up, they were eight feet tall, and they had pincers the size of antlers. They weren't mindless monsters, though. They played music. Do the centipedes of Earth play music, Bradley?"

He shook his head in response.

"Well these ones did. We never saw them do it, mind. I don't know whether they had instruments, or sawed their legs together like grasshoppers, or what. It was a terribly sad sound—like a chorus of cellos—but very beautiful."

He eased back into his chair with a faraway look in his eyes.

"I remember that campaign well," he said with a smile. "We would fight all day on the tundra, and at night, we would hear this beautiful music playing in the distance. Oh, but they were fierce opponents, those centipedes! There were times when I honestly didn't know how we would beat them."

He lit the cigarette. It crackled and popped, filling the air with blue fumes.

"So how *did* you beat them?" asked Bradley.

Lord Victor exhaled very slowly, until all the smoke had left his lungs.

"We just kept going," he said at last, "until we'd killed every last one of them."

He peered at the glowing end of his cigarette.

"I wish I'd recorded that music, Bradley. It's gone forever. You can't hear it anywhere in the universe—but I suppose that," he finished, with a humourless smile, "is how we do business on Mars. We're not a sentimental people, you know."

Bradley didn't know what to say to that, so he didn't say anything. He could hear a clock ticking somewhere behind him.

After a while, Lord Victor reached for his newspaper.

"Well it was a pleasure meeting you," he said with a cold smile. "And I'm sure we'll meet again. I'd like to hear more about your blue whale."

Bradley nodded and scurried off. When he got to the common room door, he paused and looked over his shoulder. The Martian billionaire was reading his paper, half-smiling— or was it the ghost of a sardonic sneer?—at something he'd found in its pages.

Bradley shuddered. Then he left the common

room and made his way to Grandpa's apartment, wondering what the night had in store for them.

PROJECT VORTEX

BEFORE LONG, THE adventurers had reconvened, donned their invisibility suits, and made their way unseen to reception.

It was very strange to be wearing an invisibility suit. For starters, when Bradley looked through the goggles, he didn't see things as they normally appeared. He could see the outlines of Grandpa and Headlice, picked out in glorious gold light. As they went on ahead of him, they looked like angels. At the same time, everything that was part of the normal visible world—from the silent orderlies to the pictures on the walls—seemed dark and unreal, like a world of ghosts.

When they got to reception, the entrance to the North Wing seemed darker and more foreboding than ever. Bradley didn't relish the thought of having to brave the Discouragers. Then something occurred to him.

"Headlice! Why don't you just *disable* the Discouragers?" he wondered out loud.

His earpiece popped and hissed.

"What do you mean?" she replied in a crackly voice. *"How?"*

"You know. You could do your weird alien brain thing."

He was thinking of a previous time—a time on a dwarf planet, far from the sun—when the three of them had been attacked by a giant robot. Headlice had used the power of her mind to frazzle the robot's circuits.

"What do you mean," she said testily, *"my weird alien brain thing?"*

"Oh, you know. Your special power. You could zap them or something with your brainwaves."

At that point, Grandpa butted in.

"Don't!" he said. *"It'll look like sabotage and draw their attention. We don't want anyone to*

know we've been snooping around."

"Well it's academic," said Headlice bitterly, *"because I can't do it anyway. I need to see them first to get a lock on them, and they're hidden from view. Sorry, Bradley. I'm sure you would have enjoyed the freak show."*

"That's all right," he said magnanimously. "Don't apologise. It's not your fault."

In the end, passing under the Discouragers wasn't as bad as he'd feared. Now that he'd done it a couple of times, the terror had dwindled to a kind of crawling unpleasantness, and entering the North Wing was no worse than walking out in a fierce downpour. It was simply a case of him putting his head down, gritting his teeth, and getting on with it.

Before long, they had reached the end of the corridor.

"Right!" said Grandpa over the radio. *"Let's explore. Which way should we go first? Left turn or right turn?"*

Before Bradley could answer, he heard footsteps behind him. They turned to see that two dark figures had entered the North Wing. At that distance, and through the gloom of the goggles, it was impossible to see who they were—but Bradley thought that one of them looked like Lord Victor.

"*Quick!*" hissed Grandpa—pressing himself flat against the wall. "*Get out of the way!*"

They did exactly that, allowing the two men to pass. As Bradley had suspected, one of them was Lord Victor. The other was a stranger, with skin whiter than fresh snow, and eyes that were bluer than a mountain lake. His swollen neck spilled over his collar, hanging down the front of his shirt like a warty cravat.

"It's very kind of you," he was saying in a deep voice, "to show me around this facility, Lord Victor."

"Not at all!" replied his host. "I haven't forgotten your generous investment in Bonneville Enterprises. I look forward to paying you an equally generous dividend from Project Vortex."

As the two men passed, Bradley felt an intense

chill wash over him. He realised that Lord Victor's guest was radiating cold air. In fact, the stranger was like a walking snowman, to the extent where tiny icicles had formed all over his face.

Grandpa—still pressed against the wall—made eye contact with Bradley through the special goggles.

"That's an Orcan!" he explained. *"They live on a tiny planet called Orcus, a long long way from the sun. Because their blood's so cold, they have a special antifreeze gland in their necks. If it ever packs up they freeze solid."*

Lord Victor escorted the Orcan to the end of the corridor. When they took a right turn, Grandpa barked an order over the radio link.

"After them!" he said.

They followed Lord Victor and his guest down a long corridor, which zigged and zagged and doubled back on itself. At last, they came to a long straight hall with doors on either side of it, facing in like two rows of cells. Each had a sliding hatch, like the kind that wardens use to check on prisoners. Groans could be heard behind some of them, which made Bradley feel uneasy.

"These are the private wards," Lord Victor explained. "We have a number of special guests who stay here, rather than in the South Wing."

"Is one of them the subject of Project Vortex?"

"Yes. There's a special, ultra-secure ward for Project Vortex. I'm taking you there now."

At the end of the corridor was another door, with a camera and speaker on the wall beside it.

"Helpotron!" said Lord Victor brightly. "This is my guest, Lord Octantis. I would like you to open the door for us."

"All right," said Helpotron unhappily. *"Come closer so I can do the retina scan."*

Lord Victor stood with his face close to the camera. Very briefly, a white flash lit up his features.

"Why do you sound so glum all the time?" he muttered. "It's very distracting!"

"Sorry boss. I just don't like being in the North

Wing.   This whole project gives me the creeps.   I'll be glad when it's over."

"Oh, don't be so ridiculous," snapped Lord Victor.   "You're a computer program—not a baby!   You're not even really here.   You're installed on a hard drive somewhere in the basement."

"But it feels *like I'm here,"* complained Helpotron—*"and that's close enough for me!"*

As soon as the scan had finished, the door unlocked with a loud CLICK!

Bradley saw an opportunity and slipped inside. Before Grandpa could follow, Lord Victor waved for Lord Octantis to enter, then went in himself.   As soon as he was through the door, it slammed behind him with a heavy metallic thump.

Bradley panicked and pressed his earpiece into his ear.

"Can you still hear me?" he asked the others.

"Just about," said Grandpa—sounding very far away.   *"What can you see in there?"*

Bradley looked around.   The private ward

wasn't that different to his own room, except for the fact that it didn't have a window. Someone was lying very still in the bed, with the white bedding pulled over his face. The sheet fluttered where his mouth would have been, showing that he was breathing. Other than that and the beeping monitor, there were no signs of life.

"It's just a room," he told Grandpa. "Hang on. Let me listen."

By that point, Lord Victor had taken his guest to the head of the bed.

"This is the specimen," he said proudly. "Would you like to see?"

The Orcan nodded, and Lord Victor lifted the sheet. Bradley couldn't see from where he was standing, but Lord Octantis could. He drew back and shuddered visibly.

"Terrifying," he said—with an approving smile. "Quite a coup for the Andromeda Club! But are we safe? What happens if he wakes up?"

"Don't worry. His arms and legs are

restrained. He can't hurt you."

"May I venture a guess as to how you came by him?"

"Certainly," said Lord Victor. "Guess away."

"Well, everyone knows that you're the richest man on Mars. And Phobos is a moon of Mars. I guess you have a controlling stake in whatever company runs the facility there, and simply arranged for one of the specimens to be sent over. Am I right?"

Lord Victor smiled at the theory.

"Nice idea," he said, "but I'm afraid there's no such company. The Space Police don't let contractors anywhere near Phobos. I spent many years trying to get a foot in the door, but it was useless."

"So how *did* you come by him?"

"By sheer fluke," admitted Lord Victor. "He ended up in the nets of one of my space trawlers."

"And what will you do with him?"

"Clone him," said Lord Victor. "Then we'll train the clones and sell them to all the armies of the Solar System. I stand to make literally *trillions* from Project Vortex. Naturally, I'll pay a handsome chunk of that into the Andromeda Club coffers—and an equally handsome dividend to you. It will be a pleasure to pay you back after all this time."

"But are you confident he can even *be* trained?"

"I think so. We've been waking him up in short bursts and trying to communicate with him. We've made some remarkable discoveries about his kind. They seem to have a phenomenal sense of smell. And they're like parrots, you know. They learn sounds and phrases and repeat them back to you. Excellent mimics. It's quite creepy."

"How funny. I wonder why they do it?"

"Just a quirk of evolution, I'm sure."

"But what if—unlike the parrot—he can't be trained to perform?"

"If he doesn't respond to encouragement, we'll see if he bows to brute force," said Lord Victor. "Brain implants, electric shocks—that kind of thing. One way or another, we'll break him."

On that ominous note, he let the sheet fall onto the patient's face.

"It's been hard keeping it under wraps," he admitted. "That's why I arranged to host the Star of Galatea here. It's the perfect excuse for high security comings and goings in the night. Little do they know that the Star of Galatea is just a distraction!"

Lord Octantis smiled coldly.

"Some distraction!" he pointed out. "The Star of Galatea—my oh my! A thousand carats of brilliant blue diamond. I believe it's priceless."

The patient stirred under his sheet, making the two lords jump in unison.

"Priceless!" he repeated—mimicking Lord Octantis perfectly. "Priceless!"

"Remarkable!" said the Orcan. "I wonder—"

"Remarkable!" echoed the patient—cutting him short. "I wonder—what happens if he wakes up? Wha—wha—wha—what happens if he wakes up?"

Then he switched to Lord Victor's voice.

"Brute force.   Brain implants.   Electric shocks," he promised darkly.

Lord Octantis looked unsettled, but his host smiled and calmed him.

"Don't worry," he said soothingly.   "He often stirs in his sleep, but he's doped up to the eyeballs.   Let's leave him for now.   Helpotron! Open the door."

They left the ward.   Bradley walked behind them, ready to leave—but to his horror, Lord Victor paused in front of the open doorway, making it impossible for him to get out.   He ducked this way and that, trying to identify a gap that he could slip through.   No such opportunity presented itself.

In the end, he had to jump out of the way as the door swung shut with a terrible CLANG!— trapping him inside.

Footsteps faded down the corridor, leaving him alone with the sleeping patient.

Eventually, his earpiece crackled.

"Bradley? Are you there?"

His heart leapt at the sound of a familiar voice. It was Grandpa.

"I am," he replied. "I couldn't get out in time. I'm locked in."

"I know. I saw. Is there another way out?"

He looked around in despair. There was some kind of vent in the ceiling. It was just about big enough to climb through, and the grille didn't look too sturdy, but it was far too high to get at.

"No," he said bleakly. "Nothing."

"Nothing at all? No kind of opening?"

"There's an air vent in the ceiling, but it's too high to get at."

"Jump."

"I told you, it's too high," he said in frustration.

"Blistering black holes! Nothing's *too high,* Bradley. *You can jump off an asteroid and never come down. It depends on how strong the gravity is."*

Bradley shook his head in annoyance.

"But the gravity's one gee," he pointed out—

beginning to get exasperated. "It's one gee everywhere in Moon House. Why would it—"

He stopped midway through the sentence. Suddenly, he knew what Grandpa meant. Back in his own room, there was a dial to adjust the gravity. Dr Oberon had told him not to use it, so he'd forgotten it was there.

"If you turn the gravity down," Grandpa told him, *"you'll be able to reach the ceiling easily. Can you do that?"*

He glanced at the wall above the bed. There! Exactly the same dial in exactly the same place.

"I'll give it a go," he promised.

He approached it cautiously. As he did, the mysterious figure stirred beneath the sheets, making his heart begin to pound. Who was under there, he wondered?

"Brain implants," said the patient suddenly—apropos of nothing.

As Bradley watched, the patient began to lurch this way and that, trying to free himself.

"Brain implants," came the voice beneath the sheet. "Brain implants. Brain implants."

Bradley found it uncanny. The patient was imitating Lord Victor so well, and so precisely, that it was hard to believe it wasn't the Martian himself under the sheet.

"Electric shocks," added the patient. "Whuh—whuh—whuh—whuh—one way or the other—electric shocks!"

Bradley shivered and reached for the dial—glad that he was invisible.

As his hand hovered over the bed, the patient tried to jerk upright.

"Some distraction!" he said—this time in Lord Octantis's voice.

He tried to sit up again and again. Each time, there was the dull glassy CHINK! of a chain being pulled taut. Then Lord Victor's voice floated up from the bed.

"They seem to have a phenomenal sense of smell," he added pointedly.

Bradley stopped dead—his outstretched arm still trembling in front of him.

The hairs rose on the back of his neck, making his skin crawl all over. A terrible thought had occurred to him.

Did the patient know he was there?

"Bradley! Have you done it?" asked Grandpa impatiently—making him jump.

He swallowed with some effort.

"Not yet," he managed. "I'm about to do it now."

With some effort, he reached for the dial and turned the gravity all the way down. Suddenly, he felt very light. So light that when he stood on his tiptoes, it took a long time for his heels to settle back onto the floor. He moved slowly away from the bed.

The patient stirred again. This time, because the gravity was much lower, the sheet billowed like it was underwater.

"What's actually in there?" wondered Headlice through the earpiece.

"That's a very good point!" agreed Grandpa. *"In the excitement of us all getting separated, I completely forgot to ask! Have you got to the bottom of Project Vortex?"*

"No," replied Bradley. "There's a patient here,

but he's hidden with a sheet."

"Look under it then."

Bradley didn't respond. Grandpa's simple instruction had gripped his heart with cold dread.

"I—I don't think I should," he said at last. "He's getting restless. And from what they were saying, I think he's pretty dangerous."

"What do you know about him?"

"Well, he's shaped roughly like you or me. I mean, he looks like he has a head and two arms and two legs. He can copy voices, like a parrot. And he has a good sense of smell."

By the time he'd finished, he could almost hear Grandpa shaking his head in bewilderment.

"Sorry Bradley. That's not enough to go on. Did they mention anything else?"

"They said they found him in the net of a space trawler. What's a space trawler?"

"It's just a ship that drags a net through space. Lord Victor has a whole fleet of them, called Bonneville Enterprises."

Bradley looked at the bed. Whoever it was

had stopped moving—but in the low gravity, ripples continued to spread as the sheet settled back onto the mattress.

"Is that it? No more clues?"

Bradley didn't answer. With the gravity turned down, the mysterious figure looked positively supernatural. It was like a white spectre, mustering dark forces as it lay fluttering in its grave...

Suddenly, he remembered something.

"I think there's more of them on Phobos," he told Grandpa. "Lord Victor said that—"

"Get out of there right now," said Grandpa.

Bradley's blood ran cold.

"What? Why? What's wrong?" he wondered.

"Now," insisted Grandpa.

Bradley glanced fearfully towards the bed. Then—moving ponderously, as if he were wading through water—he positioned himself under the hatch with the flimsy-looking grille.

"Okay," he said. "I'm going to try jumping."

The gravity was so low that, when he bent his knees, he didn't quite squat. Both of his feet

143

simply lifted off the ground, leaving him to sink downwards after a short delay.

It was no use trying to hurry, but he wanted to. He was painfully aware that the patient was beginning to stir again.

"Have you done it?" asked Grandpa. *"Don't dawdle in there, whatever you do!"*

"I won't, I promise. I'm going as fast as I can."

At last, his feet were firmly back on solid ground. Without waiting a moment longer, he kicked both legs at once, propelling himself skyward like a rocket.

The minute he did, he realised that he'd overdone it. He managed to cover his head, just in time for him to smash the grille with his elbows.

It popped out of the hatch, making a ferocious racket as it bounced around in the duct above. Sadly, Bradley was too busy protecting his head to catch hold of anything. Feeling slightly stunned, and with his forearms smarting at the impact, he simply sank back down to the floor.

The minute he did, he realised that he wasn't alone.

The mystery patient was wide awake now, roused by the sound of the breaking grille. He thrashed this way and that, causing the sheet to rise up into the air. His chains rattled and slapped against the mattress.

"Bradley!" cried Grandpa over the radio. *"What's happening in there?"*

He didn't answer. Instead, he panicked at the sight of the dancing bedding and jumped again.

This time, he had enough command of his limbs to grab the edge of the hatch and haul himself up into the ceiling.

Before his head vanished into the darkness, he got a glimpse of the patient's hand.

A powerful, grasping grey hand that he remembered well.

"Bradley?"

There came a crisp loud SNAP! as one of the patient's chains shattered.

Links flew in all directions, rolling through

145

the air like little meteors. As they began to strike the walls, Bradley wriggled through the narrow hatch and into a long duct, crawling away as fast as he could.

FLYING SOLO

BRADLEY HAD SEEN that grasping grey hand before.

He pressed his earpiece, pushing it deep into his ear as he lay in the dark.

"Grandpa?" he said. "Can you hear me?"

The only answer was white noise. He might as well have been pressing a seashell to his ear.

"Grandpa? It's one of the pirates," he said desperately. "Can you hear me? I—I saw its hand."

Finally, a wavering reply floated back from the static.

"*Yes,*" said Grandpa tensely. "*I know. Phobos is the maximum security facility where captured pirates go. There aren't any guards on the surface because it's too dangerous. They just dump the pirates there, to live off whatever they can find or catch.*"

"Right," said Bradley grimly. "And now one's come to Moon House."

He craned his neck, trying to listen. Luckily, after snapping one of the chains, the patient seemed to have settled down again.

He remembered how the pirates had attacked them near Pluto. Then his eyes widened.

Of course!

One of them—the ringleader, with the white scar—had gone tumbling away into space.

"I think it's one we met before," he told Grandpa. "Remember? The one who fell. I guess he kept on falling until he landed in that net."

He strained to hear the reply. He could tell that Grandpa was talking, but couldn't make out the words.

There was a pause, and then Grandpa tried again.

"*—get you out of there,*" he finished suddenly. "*After that, we need to skedaddle. I don't know* what's going on at Moon House, but I don't want to be under the same roof as that thing. Can you see a way out?"

"Not really. It's dark. I'm in a kind of ventilation duct. I need to see where it goes."

"Sorry?"

"I said, not really! Can you hear me? I need to see where this duct goes."

"All right. We're still standing by the door. You're almost out of range, so when you start exploring, we'll lose contact. I'm afraid you're on your own."

"Good luck!" added Headlice in a small voice.

"What? Now hang on!" said Bradley. "If that's the case, I'll stay right where I am. I don't want us to lose contact."

There was an awkward silence at the other end.

"But then Headlice and I would have to stay put too," said Grandpa. "And we can't help you from here. We need to come up with a plan and actually do something. We're going to go back to the—"

The connection dissolved into static again.

Since he couldn't hear Grandpa, Bradley took the opportunity to remove the earpiece and listen out for the pirate stirring. Luckily, he couldn't hear a thing.

When he replaced the earpiece, Grandpa was talking again.

"—must come out somewhere. Are you still there? Hello?"

"I'm still here."

"Good. Now listen. You need to look for a way out. While you do, we'll try to come up with a way of helping you. If the worst comes to the worst, we'll confide in Dr Oberon during the big party tonight. Lord Victor will be distracted by all that stuff with the Star of Galatea. Speak soon, okay?"

Bradley responded with alarm.

"Speak soon?" he said in disbelief. "You mean—you mean you're leaving me?"

"Listen, Bradley, I'm sorry. I really am. But if you want to be a space explorer like me, you need the confidence to fly solo during a crisis. So find a way out of there. If there isn't one, then you need to keep calm, because panicking won't help any of *us—will it?"*

"Don't worry!" added Headlice. *"We won't abandon you!"*

Bradley didn't know what to say to either of them.

"But—but you sort of *are* doing," he managed at last. "Aren't you?"

"We're what, sorry?"

He removed his goggles and rubbed his eyes in frustration. He felt totally and utterly helpless.

Then he remembered how proud he'd been—back in the orbiting hospital—when Grandpa had told him what he'd said to Dad.

"Okay," he agreed. "I'm not going to panic. I'll do my best to find a way back to you. Okay?"

"Good lad," said Grandpa—and then he said no more.

After the line went dead, Bradley put his goggles back on and took stock of his situation. The hatch with the smashed grille was only a short way behind him. However, he would struggle to get over it feet-first, so decided to carry on in the direction he was pointing.

He wriggled along like a soldier in a trench. The duct was a long square tunnel with metal sides. It was there to let air circulate between different rooms, but it was big enough for him to crawl through quite comfortably. That was lucky.

Another small mercy was the fact that he had just enough light to see. At regular intervals, there would be a grille to let air in and out of the duct. Whenever there was, light would shine up from the room below. There wasn't much of it, but once his eyes adjusted to the gloom, he found that he could progress with a reasonable amount of confidence.

Unfortunately, that was the end of his good fortune. The rooms below were deserted, so he couldn't call for help. Nor could he prise any of the grilles from their hatches. Pounding on them didn't achieve anything either. Clearly, only his prodigious skyward momentum had dislodged the first one.

To make matters worse, after a while of exploring, his invisibility suit began to run out of helium. Soon, he was no more invisible than you or me. He cursed his bad luck and continued down the duct.

Eventually, it widened suddenly to make a sort of room. Mercifully, this was big enough to stand up in. There was some kind of unit mounted on the wall, which (like so many of the things in Moon House) had one of Helpotron's speakers embedded beside it. The unit was dotted with green and red lights, which made enough of a glow to see by.

Bradley straightened and looked around. As far as he could tell, he'd found an access point for maintenance workers. There was a trapdoor at his feet, but when he tried to lift it, he heard the rattle of a padlock underneath. A sponge and plastic bucket had been left in the corner.

Luckily, the service area wasn't a dead end. A second duct led away from it, sloping gently downwards. He got on his front and wriggled into it. When he guessed that he was somewhere around the height of the floor, it levelled out and turned a corner.

His guess turned out to be correct. The next grille that he came to was in the side of the duct, rather than on the bottom as previous ones had been. When he looked through it, he got a worm's eye view of a very gloomy kitchen. The main lights were off, but some had been left on overnight.

He squinted through the grille. The staff hadn't done a very good job of cleaning up for the night. One of the cupboards had been left open, exposing the dull metal gleam of pots and pans. On the surface directly above it, he could see a stack of saucers, a half-empty wine bottle, several teacups, and a box with a picture of Jupiter on the side.

He gave the grille a good whack. It was totally immobile.

He continued and came at last to the end of the duct. There was one more grille for him to investigate. When he looked through it, he saw a large room full of tables and chairs. There was a stage with a microphone and an enormous chandelier hanging over it. The lights were off, but everything was lit by a ghostly blue glow from an unseen window.

His heart leapt. The Andromeda Ballroom! What a stroke of luck! Everyone would be there that evening. Surely he could exploit that fact?

But the more he thought about it, the less he thought he could. *Everyone* would be there. It wasn't like he could wave Grandpa over for a quick chat through the grille.

He flipped onto his back and pinched the bridge of his nose, desperately trying to concentrate—but it was no good. It was too hot and stuffy to think clearly.

He wriggled around, trying to remove the outer layer of his invisibility suit. Since he'd run out of helium, it had just been a source of discomfort to him. Eventually, he managed to slip out of it, like a snake shedding its skin.

Once the outer layer was off, he felt much cooler and more relaxed, and better able to formulate a plan.

At last, he remembered something. It hadn't seemed seemed relevant at the time, but the more he thought about it, the more striking it seemed.

Gradually, the ghost of a plan began to form in his mind.

He smiled in the darkness. It wasn't the best plan ever, but it *was* a plan, and he had a sudden strong hunch that it would work a treat.

He inched his way back to the service area, feet-first.

The minute he emerged from the duct, he stood up and stretched. He used the space to fold his invisibility suit and place it neatly in the corner. Then he put his face very close to the speaker by the unit on the wall.

"Helpotron," he whispered. "Helpotron! You know I'm here, don't you? I bet you've known all along."

"*I certainly have!*" said the speaker brightly. "*I know the location of every guest in Moon House!*"

Bradley nodded.

"Right. You told me that before, and it came back to me just this second. I didn't know whether you could track us when we were invisible, but then it occurred to me that I ran out of helium anyway. Have you reported me to Lord Victor?"

"Nope!" said Helpotron.

"How come?"

"Well basically, I just don't like him very much."

Bradley smiled to himself.

"Then I want you to do me a favour," he said. "A favour to spite Lord Victor."

Helpotron didn't seem sure.

"Error. Did you mean—"

"Don't pretend," said Bradley firmly. "I know you understand me. You're not as daft as you make out."

"Look," pleaded the speaker. *"I'm in a difficult position. Lord Victor's voice is literally hardwired into my circuits. Do you understand? If he asks me a direct question, he gets an honest answer. If he gives me a direct order, I can't resist. That's*

how it works."

"I get it. But that won't be a problem. Will there be music at Lord Victor's party?"

"*Yes.*"

"Okay. Good. In that case, I need you to get a message to Grandpa."

"*I can't.*"

Bradley was surprised.

"You can't? Are you kidding? Lord Victor told you not to?"

"*No. But your Grandpa isn't near any of my speakers. He's trying to abseil down the side of Moon House with a load of bedding tied together.*"

"Why?"

"*I have literally no idea. I think he's trying to help you somehow.*"

"All right. Well, what about Headlice?"

"*I can get a message to Headlice. She's in her room. What should I say?*"

"The message is this. At the party—when the music starts playing—she needs to come to the kitchen. I'll tell her what to do through the grille near the floor. Can you do that?"

"*No problem. But why not get her to come to the grille right now?*"

"Because I've got a plan that will make a lot of noise. I need everyone to be distracted and I need the music to drown it out."

"*Fine. I'll tell her.*"

Bradley nodded, then yawned. Suddenly, his eyes felt very heavy. It had been a very long night, he realised, and he was overdue some beauty sleep.

"Thanks," he said. "Well—that's it for now. Wake me up if anything happens. Okay?"

Having said which, he wriggled into the dark of the ventilation duct, rested his head on his hands, and fell fast asleep—soothed by the sound of the air conditioning.

THE JUPITER TEA PARTY

BRADLEY WOKE TO the sound of activity.

He went to both grilles to do some spying.
In the Andromeda Ballroom, Lord Victor was
supervising a comprehensive clean-up operation.
He stood on the raised stage, giving orders to
an army of cleaners from beneath the enormous
chandelier.

At the same time, in the kitchen, cooks were
slaving away at enormous ovens, filling the air
with the percussive sounds of kitchenware being
jostled and scraped and banged. Clearly, they
were getting things ready for the big party.

Suddenly, Bradley realised that he'd made a
big mistake. He should have got Headlice to
come during the night. Even if they hadn't put
his plan into action there and then, she could at

least have given him a drink of water through the grille. He hadn't thought of that, and now he was very thirsty.

More urgently, his bladder was full to bursting. He tried to ignore it, but in the end, he had to go back to the little service area and use the bucket that had been left there.

This did not go without being noticed.

"Blimey!" said Helpotron quietly. *"First the sink—now a bucket! You're a peeing maniac!"*

"I was desperate!" protested Bradley. "It's not my fault! Do you know where I can get a drink of water?"

"Yes," said Helpotron surprisingly. *"The thing on the wall is a dehumidifier. If you open it up, you can drink the water that's collected in the bottle. Don't pee in it though."*

Bradley wasn't sure.

"We've got a dehumidifier at home," he said. "It's got a sticker on that says you shouldn't drink the water because it might have microbes in."

"But this is a special *dehumidifier,"* Helpotron

assured him. *"Water's very precious on the moon. We can't afford to waste a drop of it. It's perfectly drinkable."*

Bradley took his word for it. Moments later, he'd thrown open the unit, unscrewed the bottle, and was greedily glugging the water. It wasn't very cold, but it was just what he needed.

"Thanks," he said when he'd finished.

After that, there wasn't much to do except lie around listening to his own stomach growling. The smells from the kitchen made his hunger doubly keen. He noticed that there was an ebb and flow to the activity. Sometimes it would be packed, sometimes it would be empty, and sometimes a couple of *chefs de partie* would get a moment alone to gossip.

Eventually, Bradley heard an imperious woman addressing the others.

"Okay. That's everything. Well done everyone. Let's set the buffet table, and then we're done for the day."

As they filed from the kitchen, he wriggled to

the end of the duct and pressed his face to the other grille. A good few minutes later, the chefs began to appear in the Andromeda Ballroom, each carrying a large metal tray of canapés. The bite-sized treats were even more extravagant than Earthling ones. There were neon pink sandwiches and glowing green samosas, and the vol-au-vents were so light and fluffy that they actually defied gravity, hovering high above the silver platters.

He didn't watch for long. Partly because he didn't want to be spotted, but mainly because he hadn't had breakfast, and the sight of all that food was making him salivate. He just lay on his back, running through the plan in his mind.

While he lay there, he listened. As the hours went by, the ballroom began to fill with people. First, he heard a couple of low voices; then a steady chatter; then an excitable din.

After what felt like a lifetime, someone tapped a microphone pointedly.

"Ladies a-a-a-a-a-a-a-and gentlemen!" began Lord Victor. "Welcome, all of you, to the

Andromeda Ballroom. The Star of Galatea is the rarest and most beautiful diamond in the universe, and to celebrate it being here, we're throwing a big party for everyone at Moon House."

There was a round of thunderous applause. Bradley was impressed by Lord Victor. He was clearly a confident speaker and commanded the crowd like a seasoned MC.

"We'll be unveiling the diamond shortly," he promised. "But first, we have a lush buffet to get through. We also have *The Music of the Spheres* by the Laser Harp Quintet. Before they take the stage, let me first introduce some special guests."

He paused for effect.

"At the table to my left, you can see the very distinguished Mr Klezop Hilfiger. He's the CEO of Gee Whiz Corporation, and he's got some free samples of a new product called *Gee Whiz Light*. It tastes of pomegranate, and just a few mouthfuls will make you totally weightless."

There was a round of polite applause for Mr

Klezop Hilfiger.

"At the same table," continued Lord Victor, while the clapping continued, "you can see a dear old friend of mine, Lord Octantis of Orca. He has commercial space fishing interests all over the Solar System."

The applause was dutifully renewed.

"At the table to my right, I'm sure you all recognise the holographic superstar Jeff Scissors, who made his millions with TV formats like *Who Wants a Massive Bag of Crisps*, *Don't Say 'Sausage'*, and *I'm Drunk, Help Me Find My Trousers*."

More applause.

"And lastly, ladies and gentlemen—can we please have another, extra-big round of applause for Otto Rastaban—founding member and lifetime president of the illustrious Andromeda Club, which has poured so much funding into Moon House."

When the crowd finished clapping, the Laser Harp Quintet began to play. Bradley crawled to the grille that served the kitchen.

It took ages for Headlice to arrive, but to his relief, she came as planned.

First, he heard the door open. Her footsteps echoed in the empty kitchen, and it wasn't long before she stepped into view.

"Headlice!" he said urgently. "Headlice! I'm down here!"

She looked around blankly, then noticed the grille near the floor. Her one eye widened when she saw him looking through the holes.

"Bradley!" she cried in delight. "It's you!"

She ran over and pushed a finger through the grille, desperately trying to make contact. Without thinking, he gave it an affectionate squeeze.

"We have to act fast," he told her. "Do you know how to boil water?"

She nodded.

"Good. Get a pan boiling, then find some sugar cubes and bring them here."

When she returned, he told her to start stacking the sugar against the vent. As it turned out, the cubes were just about small enough to pass through the grille. He got her to feed some through the holes and began to stack them from the other side.

At first, she was committed and industrious. Then she began to slow down.

"Bradley?" she said.

"What?" he wondered—beavering away.

She watched him through the grille. Then her gaze returned to the pile of sugar cubes that grew between them.

"Are you having a nervous breakdown?" she asked eventually.

"No! Why?"

"Well I thought I was meant to be helping you escape," she explained. "But instead, you've got me boiling water and making a fort out of sugar cubes."

"It's not a fort. It's a bomb."

That settled it. She stood up decisively.

"Stay here," she told him. "I'm getting Grandpa."

"What?! No, listen. There's something called *Jovian Tea.* It comes from Jupiter, and it explodes when you add sugar. I saw it happen in the common room. Is the water boiling yet?"

"Yes."

"Okay. This is the plan. You need to find some Jovian teabags and drop them in the water. Then you're going to spill the tea on the floor. You need to get out of the way before it reaches the sugar. I'm banking on it blowing a hole in the grille. Oh—and there's a box somewhere behind you," he added, "with a picture of Jupiter on it. I saw it before. Try that. It might be the tea."

She quickly located and opened the box

"Teabags!" she reported with delight.

His heart began to pound. They were rapidly approaching the moment of truth. He watched her make the tea and set the pan on the floor. Satisfied that it was all going to plan, he wriggled well away from the grille.

"Okay," she called. "I'm spilling it now."

He heard a splash, followed immediately by her rapid retreating footsteps. He pictured the tea creeping towards the sugar—advancing like a mudslide...

He began to wonder how long it would take. Before the thought even got chance to form itself, there was a terrifying BANG! that made him cringe and cover his head.

"It worked!" cried Headlice, when the dust had settled.

He wormed his way back to the grille. He was delighted to see that the tea had blown a massive hole in the bottom of it. The force of the explosion had spattered the interior of the duct with caramelised sugar, leaving a strong smell of sweet popcorn. Outside the hatch, any crystals that hadn't exploded were spread across the kitchen tiles, making them sparkle like granite.

"Brilliant!" he said—pulling the remains of the grille out and tossing them aside. "Now help me through this hatch."

Once he was free of the duct, he straightened and stretched. Then he waited awkwardly while she threw her arms around him, engulfing him in a bear hug.

"Okay—enough of that," he decided—firmly freeing himself from Headlice's arms. "We need to get out of here, before someone discovers we blew a hole in the wall."

Then he remembered something and face-palmed himself in frustration.

"I left my invisibility suit behind," he told her. "What an idiot! I need to get it. Then I'll rescue Grandpa from that party. You go to my room and get Waldo. We'll all meet up in reception. Okay?"

She gave him a dazzling smile and ran off. As he wriggled back into the duct, he felt a sudden rush of joy. Only a few moments ago, he'd been trapped in the walls. Grandpa had challenged him to find a way out, and he'd risen to that challenge. Now it was time to ditch Moon House for good.

By the time he popped his head into the little service area, he was beginning to smile at his own brilliance. So much so, in fact, that it took him a second to register that someone—or rather *something*—was standing before him.

Bradley looked up, absorbing the stocky shape of the silhouette—the powerful shoulders—the distinctive conical head.

At last, he saw the faint grey gleam of the pirate's teeth.

His blood ran cold.

It had escaped!

The pirate began to moan, swaying like a zombie. Bradley was rooted to the spot with fear. Perhaps it was still half-asleep? Or maybe even sleepwalking?

"Brute force," muttered the pirate—copying Lord Victor's phrase from the previous day. "Brute force."

All at once, it exploded into motion—trying to grab him. He gasped and vanished back into the duct, then scrabbled away as fast as he could. Because the duct was too narrow to turn around, he had to go feet-first, propelling himself with his hands.

The pirate got down on its front and started to follow. Bradley could hear it banging the sides of the duct as it gave chase. When it snarled in the distance, he imagined its hot breath on his face.

He went faster and faster, but it was gaining on him. Finally, he passed the vent that served the kitchen. Light flooded in through the opening, revealing the terrifying face of the pirate for the first time.

Bradley's blood froze. It froze so hard and so fast that he half-expected his arteries to burst, like water pipes in cold weather.

The pirate looked exactly like it did in his memories—his nightmares. It had a grey conical head, with two round eyes like bottomless pits. A jagged white scar ran between them, pointing the way to its razor sharp teeth.

Bradley was done for. He didn't have time to wriggle out into the kitchen. The opening was too tricky to navigate. The pirate would be on him in a flash.

He carried on down the duct, knowing that he would reach a dead end but intending to reach it all the same. He didn't know why. Maybe he was just buying time and hoping for a miracle.

If he was, he got one.

As he shot round a corner, he realised that the pirate had fallen behind. He could still hear it thumping around, but it was nowhere near as close as it had been.

He stopped to listen, barely daring to hope.

Then he heard metal tearing. It dawned on him that the pirate wasn't giving chase. It was escaping into the kitchen. Being larger than Bradley, it was having to wrestle with the vent to widen it—but that was short work for such a strong creature. It was like a powerful square peg, forcing its way through a round hole.

Bradley couldn't believe his luck. Very quietly, he crawled on his elbows to peer around the corner. He was just in time to see the pirate's boots vanish through the opening.

He wondered where it was going.

Then—as if in answer—the pirate began to talk to itself. First in Lord Victor's voice, and then in that of Lord Octantis. The words floated from the kitchen and down the long duct, reaching Bradley as he lay exhausted in the gloom.

"The Star of Galatea," it was saying. "The Star of Galatea."

WHAT MARTIANS ARE MADE OF

As soon as Bradley emerged from the grille, he could hear people running and screaming. The pirate must have been detected by then because Moon House was being evacuated. A siren wailed above the sound of the stampede.

When Bradley left the kitchen, he found himself in a maze of service corridors. He looked around frantically for one of Helpotron's speakers but couldn't see any.

"Helpotron?" he called uncertainly. "Are you there?"

There was a pause.

"Yes," came the distant reply.

"Where are Grandpa and Headlice?"

"In the Andromeda Ballroom."

Bradley cursed the pair of them. They hadn't

got to reception yet. He made his way through the corridors until he found a familiar hall with faux-Earthling décor. Very quickly, he had to flatten himself against the wall so people could hurry past him.

Bringing up the rear was Dr Oberon.

"Bradley!" he said in surprise. "Why aren't you evacuating? Haven't you heard there's an intruder?"

"It's not an intruder," said Bradley quickly. "It's a pirate that escaped from the North Wing. Lord Victor wanted to clone it."

Dr Oberon looked surprised, then livid.

"I *knew* no good would come of the Andromeda Club," he said with contempt. "Now come on. We're evacuating. The fire exit is down here."

Dr Oberon led the way. Bradley made as if to follow, then doubled back on himself and legged it in the opposite direction. Before he reached the Andromeda Ballroom, he bumped into Lord Victor, who'd come from a different corridor but seemed to be heading the same way.

"Lord Victor!" said Bradley in surprise.

In one of his hands, the Martian billionaire held a glittering key. He held it so tightly that his red fist had turned a pale pink. The minute Bradley spotted it, he took fright and held it protectively above his head.

"Don't touch it!" he said in alarm. "It'll disintegrate!"

Despite the urgency of the situation, Bradley was curious.

"Why? What is it?"

"It's the key for the diamond," said Lord Victor. "It opens the display case."

"Why will it disintegrate?"

Lord Victor looked annoyed at the interruption.

"A security measure. If you aren't an authorised key-holder, it turns to powder in your hands. Now out of my way. I need to retrieve the diamond!"

"I'll come with you," said Bradley. "Grandpa and Headlice are still in there."

But Lord Victor pulled a face.

"Your two friends? I don't think they are. They were among the first to leave—I'm sure of it!"

When they reached the ballroom, Lord Victor threw the double doors open and strode across the lush dark carpet. Shining before them, on the stage below the enormous chandelier, was the Star of Galatea.

It was so beautiful that, when Bradley saw it, it took his breath away. It didn't resemble an Earth diamond. It shone like a blue star, throwing out rays of its own strange light.

"Wow," whispered Bradley—slowly stepping into the room.

Then he realised that the place was deserted.

"Where *are* Grandpa and Headlice?" he wondered irritably.

"*In the Andromeda Ballroom,*" said Helpotron behind him.

He turned, expecting to see a speaker. Instead, he came face-to-face with the pirate, which had been standing right behind him.

"*The Andromeda Ballroom!*" it said again—

mimicking Helpotron perfectly.

Bradley turned and ran, shouting for Lord Victor to do the same. Lord Victor—who'd been trying to unlock the diamond's display case—seemed annoyed rather than scared. He placed the key on top of the case and reached angrily into his pocket.

"I've had enough of you!" he told the pirate fearlessly.

Suddenly, Bradley glimpsed the military man of old. The ageing billionaire was gone, and in his place stood the intrepid captain who had conquered the South Pole of Mars.

"Come here, you space devil," continued Lord Victor, "and I'll show you what Martians are made of!"

He produced something that was instantly familiar to Bradley, although he was surprised to see that Lord Victor had one. It was a *Brain-O-Matic Super-Tap:* a gizmo that looked like a bathroom tap, with an ergonomic rubber grip and crazy flashing lights. Before leaving Earth, Grandpa had used one to stun Grandma and wipe her memory—and now Lord Victor was going to try the same trick on the pirate.

He closed in, twisting the top of the tap. The pirate backed away.

"Helpotron!" it said unexpectedly—using Lord Victor's voice. "Halve the gravity! Halve the gravity!"

Suddenly, Bradley felt very light. Lord Victor looked surprised and fumbled the Brain-O-Matic Super-Tap. It floated away as if through water.

Then the pirate pounced, attacking with lightning speed.

Before Lord Victor could react, it hit him with a sickening uppercut, planting its fist right beneath his ribs. He sailed high into the air and hit the ceiling.

"Set gravity to high!" ordered the pirate.

In a flash, Lord Victor was yanked from the air and thrown back down, landing with a hard THUMP!

He might as well have been fired at the floor from a cannon. Incredibly, he wasn't dead. He managed to lift his head from the carpet.

"Helpotron," he said weakly. "Lower the—"

"Don't lower the gravity," said the pirate—in exactly the same voice. Lord Victor lapsed into silence, lacking the strength to issue a counter-order.

At the same time, Bradley was on all fours, struggling to support himself against the intense gravity. Remaining in that position, he tried to crawl towards the exit.

The pirate was the only one still standing. With some effort, it went purposefully after Bradley—one step at a time, almost shuffling; every tendon like a steel cable.

Bradley looked over his shoulder. In the pirate's eyes, he thought he could detect the ghost of an emotion. It was like a cold kind of anger. It had a score to settle.

When the pirate caught up with him, it stamped brutally on his back. Bradley screamed in surprise and pain, then sank face-down on the floor. That done, the pirate shuffled back towards the stage, where the Star of Galatea shone with its terrible beauty.

Bradley lay on his front and panted lightly. He knew that he'd been properly injured. It felt like something had burst or broken inside him. His face was damp with cold sweat, and he wondered if he was going to puke or even die. Carefully, he rolled himself over so he could see the stage.

"I know why you're here," said the pirate to itself—this time in an unfamiliar voice—"but I assure you, we have nothing of value!"

Bradley wondered who it was mimicking, and then realised it could be anyone. The pirate must have heard many things during its life. He had no idea what it chose to repeat, or why.

"Please don't hurt me!" added the pirate—in a different voice again. Then it screamed, and the scream stopped suddenly. Bradley realised, with a chill, that he might have been hearing someone's last words.

He lay there in silence. Eventually, he found the strength to slither to the edge of the ballroom. One of Helpotron's speakers was embedded in the wall above him, so he turned to face it.

"Helpotron," he croaked pathetically. "Helpotron. You've got to turn the gravity back down. I'm too weak to get up. I'm going to die here."

"*Sorry Bradley,*" said Helpotron, with genuine regret. "*As far as I'm concerned, Lord Victor said not to lower the gravity. I'm powerless to disobey.*"

Bradley groaned in exasperation.

"But that *wasn't* Lord Victor!" he complained. "It was the pirate! It can do voices!"

"*I know. But it doesn't matter. Lord Victor's voice is hardwired into my circuits. I told you that before. I can't resist it. I'm sorry, Bradley. I really am.*"

Bradley resigned himself to watching the pirate. It had reached the stage now. Bathed in light from the Star of Galatea, its evil eyes shone like sapphires. It picked up the key, which—just as Lord Victor had promised—became useless powder in its hands.

It seemed surprised. Then it grunted in annoyance, made a fist, and began to punch the display case with all its might.

"The Star of Galatea!" it roared. "The Star of Galatea!"

It struck once—twice—a third time. Soon, its knuckles were covered in sticky black liquid. Tarry splat-marks covered the glass. Bradley realised that the black fluid was probably the pirate's blood—but if it felt any pain, it showed no sign of it.

"Brute force!" it cried.

Bradley's eyes began to wander. Directly over the stage, the chandelier was swinging lightly. What a shame, he thought sadly, that it wouldn't just fall and land on the pirate. Under all those shimmering crystals, it had a heavy frame that would trap anyone.

"Brute force!" said the pirate again.

As it pummelled the glass, it suddenly dawned on Bradley that the chandelier *might* fall. It must have doubled, tripled, maybe even quadrupled in weight in the intense gravity. In fact, it seemed to be straining its cable like a bungee cord...

In a flash, something occurred to Bradley.

"Helpotron," he managed quietly.

"Yes?"

"Did Lord Victor tell you not to *increase* the gravity?"

"Error! Did you—"

"I'm going to kill you if you don't give me a straight answer."

"Okay, okay. The answer is no."

"Good. Then do it. Increase the gravity."

"Are you sure? You're in a bad way. Too much gravity can be fatal, you know!"

"I know. Do it anyway."

He continued to watch the pirate. As he did, he began to feel heavier. It was as if more and more weights were being piled on top of him. He gasped in pain as his back was pressed harder onto the floor, aggravating whatever injury he'd suffered.

Soon, every breath was an effort. Incredibly, the pirate was still standing. It drew back its arm like a boxer, then delivered a last crushing blow to the display case.

With a sharp popping sound—a sound so thin it was almost a gasp—the case finally shattered. It exploded into a thousand bright pieces.

"Priceless!" cried the pirate—reaching for the huge diamond. "Priceless!"

Bradley felt light-headed. He was beginning to wobble on the edge of unconsciousness. Before his eyes, the pirate lifted the Star of Galatea.

Directly above, the chandelier trembled on its cord.

"Do you want me to stop?" asked Helpotron.

Bradley managed to shake his head.

"More weight," he whispered.

As the pirate crowed, plaster began to crack overhead—all around the base of the chandelier. Dust came down like a wisp of smoke. The pirate didn't notice. It continued to study the diamond—turning it this way and that, hypnotised by the many-angled light that seemed to burn within.

At last, as the gravity intensified, its legs began to buckle. It lowered itself onto one knee, struggling to keep the diamond off the ground...

And then it happened.

With a deep musical tone—like someone plucking the thickest string of a bass guitar—the cord that supported the chandelier snapped in two. It fell on top of the pirate, scattering dark crystals everywhere.

Eventually, a low groan came from under the chandelier. The pirate wasn't dead, but it was certainly hurt—trapped by the ornate limbs of the fallen chandelier. Some of them were covered in black splatter.

It tried to escape, but it was no good. At last, it sighed and sank into unconsciousness— leaving Bradley alone in the deserted ballroom.

A SONG OF CENTIPEDES

HE HAD NOTHING to do except lie there—trying not to move. If he didn't breathe too deeply, the pain in his lower back was just about bearable.

He began to nod off. Before long, as he swam in and out of consciousness, he wondered whether he was dreaming. He could hear voices. Dr Oberon said something in a low voice—then added, *"Remarkable—he's out cold—trapped under it!"* Grandpa said something in reply, but Bradley didn't catch it.

Then he saw Grandpa's face looking down at him, and realised that he must have been dreaming after all. The old man was standing there quite happily, as if the gravity wasn't a problem.

"*You've* been through the wars," he noted drily—with a note of pride in his voice. "Would you like something to drink?"

Bradley just smiled and nodded. If he was dreaming, he was perfectly happy to play along.

"Righty-ho," said Grandpa. "I've got just the ticket."

He strolled effortlessly round to the other side of him and knelt down. Bradley heard the pop and hiss of a can being opened by his head. Then Grandpa fed him two tablets and carefully poured the drink into his mouth so he could swallow them.

He coughed but managed to get the tablets down. They tasted sugary and sharp at the same time, like citrus fruit. The drink that came with was like cream soda with a touch of pomegranate.

As soon as the pills were in Bradley's stomach, a strange warmth spread through his body. It was a weird bubbly feeling, spreading to the tips of his toes and every finger. He realised that he was no longer in pain. Stranger

189

still, the gravity was diminishing with every second, until he was perfectly able to sit up.

He did so, then looked around in astonishment.

"I'm not dreaming!" he said groggily. "Am I?"

Grandpa smiled and shook his head.

"So what did you give me?"

"Two things," said Grandpa—and he revealed both of them. In one hand, he held a tub labelled *Mooncat's Multi-Purpose Miracle Pills.* In the other, he held a can of something called *Gee Whiz Light.*

Bradley remembered the pills from his first encounter with the pirates. Whatever injury he had, he realised, the pills would have fixed it.

Then he looked at the can. *Gee Whiz Light* sounded familiar, but he couldn't remember why.

"It's a new *anti-gravity drink,*" explained Grandpa—giving it a light shake. "A brand new product. One of the guests is from Gee Whiz Corporation, and he brought some free samples.

A few swigs counters the effect of the increased gravity. Can you stand?"

Bradley got up off the floor and grinned.

"I can!" he declared. "It works! It really does! So let's get out of here," he suggested, making for the door, "before it wears off!"

"Not so fast," said Dr Oberon behind him.

Bradley turned to see a vignette of destruction. The chandelier was smashed all over the stage with the pirate still trapped under it. A little way from that, Dr Oberon was studying Lord Victor's face. The Martian billionaire had been roused—barely—and was groaning softly.

"He's in a bad way," said Dr Oberon grimly. "I need five hundred milligrams of your Omnisolveremol."

Grandpa looked blank, so the doctor rephrased the request.

"Two pills of—what was the brand name?— *Mooncat's Multi-Purpose.* The active ingredient is Omnisolveremol."

"I'll take your word for it," agreed Grandpa— rushing over with the tub of pills.

Bradley followed him to watch. Grandpa administered the dose, but before he gave Lord Victor anything to drink, the Martian pulled a face and spat the pills back out.

"What are you trying to feed me?" he croaked. "They taste like rotten mushrooms!"—and then his eyes glazed over, and he was no longer conscious of his surroundings.

Bradley was surprised. To him, the tablets had been quite tasty. Grandpa and Dr Oberon shared an unhappy look.

"*That's* a bad sign," said Grandpa. "They're meant to taste like oranges and lemons."

"That's what they taste like when they're working," explained the doctor. "If they taste rotten, it means he's too badly injured for the treatment to work."

Then Lord Victor came round again.

"Where is the earth boy?" he demanded hoarsely. "I want to speak to him."

Bradley looked at Grandpa and Dr Oberon in alarm.

"I'm here," he replied. "Why?"

"I can't see you."

Bradley knelt close to the Martian's head.

"I really *am* here," he assured him.

But Lord Victor looked right at him, blinking blindly.

"I *still* can't see you," he complained. "Are we—are we on a spaceship?"

Bradley's heart sank. He realised that Lord Victor—who, for all his faults, had faced the pirate without a trace of fear—was in a very bad way indeed.

"Yes," he told him kindly. "Yes, we're on a spaceship. We can go wherever you want. We can go to Earth," he added—remembering their first conversation in the common room—"and see the blue whale, if you like."

But Lord Victor shook his head.

"I want to fly *backwards in time,*" he whispered absurdly. "I—I want to go to the South Pole of Mars—when I was a still a captain."

Grandpa cleared his throat.

"Plotting a course now," he said quietly—and then he shrugged at the others, as if to say, *Well what else can we do?*

There was a pregnant pause.

"Ah! Here we are," whispered Lord Victor at last—staring at the ceiling. "Can you see it sparkle? Beyond the barren plain, among the mountains—that's the mother lode! Good clean ice, ready to be mined. That's what we're fighting for, boys."

Then he gasped.

"I can hear them!" he reported with delight. "Can you? Oh, what beautiful music they make! So happy and sad at the same time. It's the centipedes, Bradley. I thought I would never hear them again. Thank you so much for bringing me here."

He breathed out slowly and didn't breathe back in again. And that—Bradley realised, kneeling quietly beside him—was the end of Lord Victor.

When they emerged, the outside of Moon House was in uproar.

Elderly guests were confronting the orderlies,

demanding to know when they would be let back inside. Others were sharing a bottle of sour mash whiskey from Old Saturn Town—which (Grandpa later told Bradley) was so strong that a mere mouthful of it would send you over the edge. The result was a drunken chorus of *Why are we waiting? We are suffocating* by the main entrance.

Bradley, Headlice, Waldo and Grandpa were soon reunited in the crowd. Headlice hugged Bradley and Grandpa, while Waldo floated around looking worried and miserable.

"I'm *so* pleased you got out of there!" said Headlice. "What happened?"

"Oh, nothing much," said Bradley modestly—but he couldn't resist adding that he'd trapped the pirate under the chandelier. Before she could express her admiration, a stranger in a blue suit came running over. He had a likeable furry face like a Scottish Terrier, with a striking pair of Buddy Holly glasses.

"Did it work?" he wondered breathlessly.

"It did!" Grandpa assured him. "Worked a

195

treat! Bradley—meet Mr Hilfiger. He's the boss of the Gee Whiz Corporation. It was Mr Hilfiger who gave us the Gee Whiz Light."

"It worked really well," agreed Bradley. "In fact—I suppose it saved my life!"

Mr Hilfiger was delighted.

"Brilliant! You couldn't *dream* of better publicity! Gee Whiz Light—saves lives! Come to think of it, you're a photogenic kid. How would you like to be the new face of Gee Whiz Soda...?"

Before Bradley could answer, Grandpa cleared his throat.

"Unfortunately," he told Mr Hilfiger—pouring cold water on the idea—"we have to return to Earth quite soon. Bradley's got school to get back to!"

At the mention of Earth, Bradley's heart—which had been so light only a moment ago—became heavy inside him. He looked up at his home planet, which shone high above their heads. In the excitement of recent events, he'd completely forgotten his predicament.

"But I *can't* go back to school," he remembered glumly. "Have you forgotten? I'm bluer than a blueberry!"

Mr Hilfiger pulled a face.

"Hardly," he pointed out. "I mean you *are* blue, but you're not *that* blue. More a sort of— pale cornflower?"

Bradley looked at his hands and realised with delight that Mr Hilfiger was quite correct. He hadn't noticed, because the change was so gradual, but the side-effects of the treatment had *definitely* faded.

Dr Oberon came floating over.

"It looks like you're returning to normal," he confirmed. "I think the side-effects will wear off completely in the coming days. In the meantime, there's no reason for you to be at Moon House. The space malaria will be completely out of your system by now, I'm sure."

Bradley laughed with joy, then gave Grandpa and Headlice a high five each. He looked up at the Earth again—seeing it, for the first time since they'd come to Moon House, with hope in his heart.

He *could* go home, he realised. He just had to wait for the rest of the blue to fade.

Then something occurred to him—something that threatened to spoil his elation. He decided not to let it. Instead, he turned to Grandpa.

"Can you bring my mum back to life?" he asked bluntly.

Grandpa looked alarmed, but Bradley pressed on.

"Do you remember—when I first met you—I said she was frozen in the loft? Well I need to know if you can bring her back to life. I've been meaning to bring it up for ages," he finished—with an intense feeling of relief.

Grandpa looked sad, but not surprised.

"I know you have," he said gently. "And I should have brought it up myself, to make it easier for you. But the fact is—and I really am sorry—but I simply can't. I don't know how. In space, you hear stories—tales around a campfire—but that's all I ever had. Stories."

He placed a hand on Bradley's shoulder and steered him away from the group.

"When I invited your father into space," he explained quietly, "I was looking for a legendary place—a comet called *Odinsaker*—where there's meant to be a cure for death. He didn't want to come, so I continued alone. That must be what your dad was thinking of, when he put your mum in suspended animation."

He sighed a deep sigh.

"I'm sorry, Bradley. I really am. But the fact is, if Odinsaker exists—I never found it. I think it's just a myth."

Bradley nodded slowly. It wasn't the answer he'd wanted, but all the same, a great weight had lifted from his shoulders. He'd finally bitten the bullet and asked.

There was a solemn pause.

"Well then!" said Grandpa at last—clapping his hands and trying to look cheery. "Are you ready to leave Moon House?"

Bradley nodded.

"Good," continued Grandpa. "Because I think

we should try to squeeze in one last adventure.
What do you say to that?"

Bradley smiled.

"One last adventure," he agreed.

And he followed Grandpa back to the group.

Farewell to Moon House

Before long, they were back on Grandpa's spaceship, speeding away from the Ocean of Storms.

The lunar plain shrank behind them. The moon—which had stretched out as far as the eye could see—became a mere snowball hanging in space.

Bradley wasn't sad to be leaving. They'd said their goodbyes to Dr Oberon, Mr Hilfiger and even Helpotron. Then they'd stopped at the Selenite camp—partly to bid farewell to the Bushwah Tribe, but also to return their invisibility suits. All in all, Bradley didn't feel like they had any unfinished business.

Now they were cruising towards Earth. Not to actually visit, of course. Just to see it, and do a quick flyover.

"Ready?" asked Grandpa.

"Yes!" said Bradley and Headlice eagerly.

They swooped in to see. The clouds and continents were barely visible through the glowing atmosphere. Then the spaceship plunged like a roller coaster. It dived down— directly down, through the blue light and wisps of cloud.

At last it levelled out. Suddenly they were racing high above marshes, mountains and slate-grey sea—fjord and forest—the sprawling grey patterns of suburbia. All of Earth passing under in a heartbeat.

Bradley held his breath, hypnotised by how beautiful it was. Then there was a loud hollow *BANG!* and the spaceship blasted back into space.

"So how was that?" asked Grandpa smugly.

"It was amazing!" gasped Headlice—watching the Earth as it shrank behind them. "Bradley! You never told me how *beautiful* the Earth is!"

"I'm only just starting to realise myself," he admitted.

While he gazed at it, Grandpa got busy at the console, pressing buttons and pushing levers.

"Right," said the old man. "That'll have to do for now. We said we were going to have one last adventure, so what will it be? We haven't seen Uranus—heh heh!—or Jupiter either—and we've barely done Neptune or Saturn—so where do you want to go?"

Bradley was glued to the porthole. Already, the Earth was racing away. It occurred to him that, of all the planets he'd seen from space, his own was the most beautiful.

He smiled—confident that he would get home eventually, and content to have one last adventure till then.

"Bradley?" pressed Grandpa.

He continued to look through the porthole. He knew that planets and asteroids were hidden out there, just waiting to be discovered. Comets, too. Maybe even one called Odinsaker...

There was room for all kinds of things in space, he thought with satisfaction.

"Surprise us!" he told Grandpa.

And off they went.

TO BE CONTINUED...

Is that the last we'll hear from the Andromeda Club? What about the bloodthirsty space pirates? Is there really such a place as Odinsaker? And will Bradley ever make it home in one piece?

You know the drill by now! Join us next time, old chums, for the FINAL THRILLING INSTALMENT of...

THE ASTRONAUT'S APPRENTICE!

ALSO AVAILABLE FROM FALCON BERGER BOOKS...

THE ASTRONAUT'S APPRENTICE

BY PHILIP THREADNEEDLE

Bradley is a normal boy who lives on a farm. One night, his long lost alien Grandpa sneaks home in a flying saucer. They embark on a whirlwind tour of Outer Space, armed with nothing but their wits, some seriously stylish space suits, and a bottle of Gee Whiz Soda. Along the way, they meet a tailor from the Asteroid Belt, a one-eyed girl from Pluto, and an exploding alien called Waldo.

Don't miss your chance to meet Grandpa—the original space-aged pensioner!

Available from major online bookstores now.

CITY OF METEORS

BY PHILIP THREADNEEDLE

In this gripping sequel to The Astronaut's Apprentice, *Bradley—a simple Earth boy—visits a secret tenth planet far from the sun. When he receives a mysterious map, he gets dragged across space by Grandpa, who wants to find the long-lost treasure of Mercury before someone else does!*

During these adventures, Bradley encounters squishy space food, hungry piranhas, and the dubious delights of the Adventurers' Emporium...

Available from major online bookstores now.

THe TRUMBLe-BUGGiNS
BY HaRRY LaDD

"OLLY AND CYNTHIA Trumblebuggins were the worst children you could ever hope to meet. You might think that you have some horrible children at your school, but in every way you can think of, and in every way that you can't, Olly and Cynthia were worse."

Naughty children are seldom popular, and between them, the Trumblebuggins children have Crackpot Juniors screaming for mercy. When they are finally expelled, their father must figure out a plan to get them back to school or else face his wife's fury. He quickly enlists the help of his drinking buddy, Mr Catchratter: a dubious genius, whose convoluted schemes leave lots to be desired...

Available from major online bookstores now.

MILTON STRANGE

AND THE ASTRAL PROJECTOR

BY MERLIN MACKINNON

Milton doesn't know much about Castle Cryptic, but finds himself drawn there all the same.

He thinks it's a summer camp for gifted children. Instead, it's a world of spells and riddles, run by magicians who work to protect us all. Their allies include Sir Marmaduke Wax—who runs a secret library in Oxford—and the Knights of the Moonlit Chamber, who beam themselves through space and time using the radio telescopes at Jodrell Bank.

Available from major online bookstores now.

5983899R00125

Printed in Great Britain
by Amazon.co.uk, Ltd.,
Marston Gate.